AFRICANA LIBRARY

Olive Schreiner

TROOPER
PETER HALKET
OF MASHONALAND

Introduced by Marion Friedmann

AD. DONKER/PUBLISHER

AD. DONKER/PUBLISHER
Craighall Mews
Jan Smuts Avenue
Craighall Park
Johannesburg
2001

Originally published in 1897 by T. Fisher Unwin, London

This edition first published 1974

ISBN 0 949937 08 8

TO A GREAT GOOD MAN
SIR GEORGE GREY

Once Governor of the Cape Colony,
who, during his rule in South Africa,
bound to himself the Dutchmen,
Englishmen, and natives he governed,
by an uncorruptible justice and a
broad humanity; and who is remembered among us today as representing
the noblest attributes of an imperial
rule.

'*Our low life was the level's and the
night's;
He's for the morning.*'

OLIVE SCHREINER

INTRODUCTION

THERE is a resurgence of interest in Olive Schreiner and this despite the fact that her work is largely inaccessible. A London borough library, although it could call on the resources of the National Central Library, could not provide me with a copy of *Trooper Peter Halket of Mashonaland.* In 1970, BBC radio broadcast a play about her; in 1971, Penguin reissued *The Story of an African Farm;* in 1973 an Olive Schreiner 'Reader' (a selection from her works called *A Track to the Water's Edge*) was published in the United States. Unpublished letters are finding their way from private ownership into university libraries in Britain and the U.S. and scholars are reportedly at work on them. But the material is not, as I've said, to hand in any sizeable quantity. Yet Olive Schreiner is being rediscovered: by Women's Libbers, socialists, pacifists, humanists, and those whose field – whatever their interest – is Africa, especially southern Africa.

That what she had to say is still relevant inclines one to pessimism: so many ideals, still to be realized. And nowhere does there seem to have been less progress than in southern Africa. In Rhodesia the scenario has barely changed. The Chartered Company has gone but the authority of the Colonial Office is still notional only. There is unfinished business demanding settlement; isolated farmhouses are on the alert for raiders in 1974 as they were in 1893 and 1896. In South Africa, too, there is unfinished business.

The vehemence and detail of Olive Schreiner's accusations against Rhodes in *Trooper Peter Halket*, the stormy course of their relationship, and even the timing – in part fortuitous – of the book's publication, have all tended to obscure the timeless quality of the book, which is an expression of a vision of the struggle between good and evil in the human heart.

Olive's relationship with Rhodes is compounded of ironies. There he is, in the Cape in the 1890s, an extraordinary man. 'When he stands on the Cape . . .,' wrote Mark Twain, 'his shadow falls to the Zambesi. He is the only colonial whose goings and comings are chronicled and discussed under all the globe's meridians . . . the only unroyal outsider whose arrival in London can compete for attention with an eclipse.' 'I am going to meet Cecil Rhodes,' Olive writes to Havelock Ellis in March, 1890, 'the only great man and man of genius South Africa possesses.' She uses the word 'genius' of him often; it denotes to her a mind somehow in harmony with the laws of the cosmos.

And there she is, in Matjiesfontein, a village some two hundred miles from Cape Town. She has returned from Europe, the celebrated author of *The Story of an African Farm*, a woman of great intellectual stature, a 'seer' with a 'dominating presence', her talk sometimes 'almost supernaturally brilliant': so South African contemporaries saw her. Rhodes has referred to *The Story of an African Farm* as a work of 'profound genius'; he often expresses a wish to meet her.

'I am more solitary than you can conceive,' she writes to Ellis in 1890, 'more lonely even than when I was a girl.' '. . . you don't know what Philistines the people in Africa are,' she writes the following month. 'I think (if) I lived fifty years in Africa I should never make one friend.' She goes on: 'There is one man I've heard of, Cecil Rhodes, the head of the Chartered Company, whom I think I should like if I could meet him; he's very fond of *The Story of an African Farm*.' In June she writes excitedly: 'I am going to Cape Town on Tuesday. I think I've told you this about ten times . . .' She has made one friend and '. . . I think I shall meet Cecil Rhodes.'

Meet they did, probably in June of that year and she writes to W. T. Stead in July (Rhodes became Prime Minister of the Cape in that

month) about the 'curious and almost pain-
fully intense interest' she feels in 'the man and
his career'. Earlier she had written about such
'curious feelings': 'These feelings never mislead
one. The person may not be great or beautiful
or good, but they are native to *you*.' And later:
'It's not love, it's not admiration . . . it's not
that I think him noble or good . . . it's the
deliberate feeling, "That man belongs to me." '
She dines often at Groote Schuur, his home; in
November and on other occasions he visits her
at Matjiesfontein. In December she travelled
up to Bloemfontein in his party for the opening
of the railway. 'He is even higher and nobler
than I had expected,' she writes, 'but our
friends are so different (that) we could never
become close friends.' In the following year she
demurs at Stead's putting her on a par with
Rhodes: 'He's much greater than I.' He is in
Mashonaland and she is anxious about him:
'Any accident to him would, I believe, mean
the putting back of our South African develop-
ment for fifty years . . .' and a month later she
writes, also to Stead, '. . . It is a bond of sympathy between us that you share my view of his
genius.'

She is angry when Rhodes votes for the
'Strop' Bill in the Cape Parliament, a Bill referred to by its Liberal opponents as the 'Every
Man Wallop His Own Nigger Bill', and is
provoked into writing a humorous skit. The

Ministers present themselves to God for admission to Heaven, and their political conduct is examined by the angels. Rhodes is consigned to Hell but the devils cannot get him into it: he is too 'great' for it; there is no room for him anywhere but in Heaven and God accepts him. The angels whisper, 'Through grace, not merit', and 'With God all things are possible'. She disapproves but can still joke: she ruefully acknowledges his stature.

The Schreiner family was deeply split over Rhodes: Olive's beloved brother Will, an eminent barrister, later a member of Rhodes's cabinet, later still Prime Minister of the Cape, stayed loyal to him until overwhelmed by evidence of his complicity in the Jameson Raid; Olive's mother was vehemently pro-Rhodes to the end. Olive traces the course of her relationship with Rhodes in letters to her mother and sister in 1896; (they are reproduced in Cronwright-Schreiner's biography). She complains (naively?) that Rhodes had, six years before, been misrepresented to her as a millionaire philanthropist, devoting his life to the downtrodden. After meeting, she said, they quarrelled violently over the 'native question' and all their meetings were of the same kind: 'we *never once* met without a royal fight'. (This is no doubt an overstatement.) All her letters to him, she insists, were an attempt to prevent his taking a downward course; she has begged him not to damn his own soul. Then he went too far: she has, she said, refused to see or greet him. 'I can afford to be quiet now,' she writes, referring to offers she has turned down for post-Jameson Raid press articles. And no doubt she meant it; she seems to have had no intention of writing *Trooper Peter Halket* which reportedly came to her 'in a flash'.

We should note that she did not believe in 'God' or 'damnation' in the orthodox sense, but in matters of profound spiritual or moral significance, she could not dispense with the metaphors.

In 1890 she had written to Ellis: 'I don't have to try not to hate anyone any more. I couldn't if I wanted to. But I can't love either.' In her letter to her mother she says and no doubt believes it: 'so far from my having hatred towards him (Rhodes) there are few men . . . for whom I have such intense sympathy'. A few months later she writes to her sister Ettie: '. . . I saw that he had deliberately *chosen* evil . . . The perception of what his character really was in its inmost depths was one of the most terrible revelations of my life.' In the same letter she speaks of 'Rhodes, with all his gifts of genius . . . and below the fascinating surface, the worms of falsehood and corruption creeping.'

'Surely,' she had asked her mother, '. . . you can distinguish between *personal* feeling and political opinions. Have they anything to do with each other?' Had they? Whether or no, a powerful head of steam was building up before 1896 and the writing of *Trooper Peter Halket*.

After the Jameson Raid she writes to a friend: 'Yes, I believe Rhodes has fallen for ever. My feelings are a strange mixture of intense personal sympathy . . . and an almost awful sense of relief that the terrible power which was threatening to crush all South Africa is broken.' She had come a long way from fearing that an accident to him would set back South Africa fifty years. (Of course, he had not 'fallen for ever': he was received, in the Cape at least, with tumultuous applause.) After the publication of *Trooper Peter Halket* she writes to Stead (July, 1897): 'You are quite mistaken as to my ever having had an unkind feeling to Rhodes; if he would only leave South Africa alone and come back to England and live in a palace and enjoy life on the money he has made out of us and our country – it's the worst I wish him!'

*   *   *

she once told my mother she would like these words only on her grave: "She wrote Trooper Peter Halket."
Lyndall Gregg: *Memories of Olive Schreiner*

(Rhodes is) worshipped by many, hated by many, but blasphemed by none among the judicious, and even by the indiscreet in guarded whispers only.

Mark Twain: *More Tramps Abroad*

'A CERTAIN distance is necessary to the seeing of great wholes clearly,' Olive Schreiner wrote in *Thoughts on South Africa*. And whenever she was concerned to express the great abstractions, she had recourse to metaphor, parable, allegory. 'I can't express myself satisfactorily didactically,' she wrote to Stead, probably in 1889. Into her allegories, Arthur Symons reported, 'she declares she puts the soul of her soul . . . she thinks them the very essence of art: all art is a symbol and these are pure symbols . . . the only artistic expression of the passion of abstract ideas, which to her are the keenest, the deepest in her nature; and in these allegories one can express humanity, not merely this man or that . . .' When, shortly before, she had re-read *The Story of an African Farm*, she had been disappointed. ' "*That* the *African Farm* – that?" But when she came to the allegory ['The Hunter'] she said: "That is right." '

The *Dunvegan Castle* left Cape Town for England in January, 1897. On board were Olive Schreiner, her husband and her brother; also on board were Cecil Rhodes and his party. The parties did not speak. She was taking the manuscript of *Trooper Peter Halket* to London for publication; he was going to face the Select Committee which was to enquire firstly into the Jameson Raid and secondly into the administration of the British South Africa Company. The Charter and thus his vision of 'extending British rule throughout the world' as his will of 1877 put it, was at risk. ('I would annex the planets if I could. I often think of that,' he is reported to have said to Stead).

'The book which I have written [*Trooper Peter Halket*] has cost me more,' she wrote in a letter, 'than anything I ever wrote, and I am broadening my back already for the Chartered Company's attacks . . .' In an unpublished letter quoted in Vera Buchanan-Gould's biography, Olive describes how she spent three days and nights almost entirely without sleep '. . . trying to decide whether I should publish it or not. I believed that Rhodes and the Chartered Company would proceed against me; I felt sure that the matter would kill me, as it did to a very large extent.' Would it, she asked herself, increase justice at all commensurate with the price she was paying? 'At length the matter decided itself within me'; her 'daemon', an instinct she trusted, told her to publish.

She sold the 'little story', she wrote to a friend in an undated unpublished letter, for £1,350. 'Did I tell you Peter Halket had been already translated into German, Swedish,

Danish, Dutch and French? . . . Of course I don't get paid for them, but the circulation of the book is the thing I care for.'

It was published in 1897 by T. Fisher Unwin while the Select Committee was in session. The first edition, with its grim photograph was followed in the same year by a popular edition, without the photograph which never reappeared.

Trooper Peter is a simple man in a company engaged in putting down the rebellion in Mashonaland in 1896. Temporarily separated from his companions, he spends the night in the veld and Christ appears to him. From his train of consciousness before Christ comes and from his dialogue with Christ, emerges a savage indictment of the Chartered Company's men. Rape, pillage, atrocity, murder, enslavement: all these charges are brought and the responsibility in large part is laid on Rhodes. In parable after parable Christ urges Peter Simon to go forth and preach His message to many auditors: men must desist from evil. But if he cannot, or is rebuffed, there is still an appeal to be made. To Rhodes, the trooper must say: '*It is never too late for the soul of a man.*' '. . . Certain sons of God are born on earth, named by men Children of Genius . . . there is laid on [each] a burden that is laid not on others . . . and if he falls beneath it, let men weep rather than curse . . .' The trooper feels his own unworthiness. Christ tells him that it is not the trumpet but the call which matters. Christ's final appeal is to Peter himself: 'In that small spot where alone on earth your will rules, bring there into being the kingdom to-day. Love your enemies . . .' The night has been Peter's road to Damascus; he rejoins his comrades, helps an African prisoner to escape and is shot for it by the Captain.

The book made a tremendous impact. Vehemence begot vehemence. *Blackwood's Edinburgh Magazine* of April, 1897, was beside itself. 'Here is a book of . . . the most immediate matters of today which comes blazing into our records, – blazing, but yet groaning and spitting like a damp torch in an access of wrath . . . beyond the power of expressing it . . . The present work is a political pamphlet of great bitterness, linked on to the very smallest thread of story that ever carried red-hot opinions and personal abuse of the fiercest kind into the world.'

There is truth in Blackwood's assertion that the story is a thin little thread and that – at one level, at any rate – the book is a political pamphlet Of the vision, Blackwood saw nothing, angered above all by the 'daring, the presumption, the folly' of Olive's introducing Our Lord, the 'extraordinary Interlocutor'. (In a fine male chauvinist flourish Blackwood notes that this is done mostly by women writers 'and it is one of the greatest evidences we know of that almost criminal recklessness . . . of which women are generally accused.') But the reviewer is uneasy about the facts: it is a 're-markable study' and 'probably gives as clear an idea of one of the wild soldiers on the borders of savagery, without principle or moral guidance . . . except a determination to grow rich, as any fiction could convey.' Whether the callousness of the soldiers is 'horrible truth or still more horrible invention, families with sons out there have an interest in knowing . . . Mr Rhodes is not our affair . . . but if our sons are trained in South Africa to be like *that* we are bound to know it and by proof that cannot be disputed.'

If the vision escapes the modern reader, an editor can do little to help him to it. Where a vision is powerful enough – I am thinking of *Animal Farm* – the reader does not ask: can and did men behave like this? But if the reader of *Trooper Peter Halket* is to respond to Olive Schreiner's vision, he cannot do so nagged by doubts about whether her indictment is by and large true.

'We cannot take Trooper Peter Halket's case before the courts. What the (imaginary) soldier said is not evidence,' wrote 'A.T.Q.C.' (Arthur Quiller Couch) in a perceptive and sympathetic review in *The Speaker* of April 3, 1897. The irony is that there was a court which could have pronounced: the Select Committee, one of whose tasks was to scrutinize the conduct of the Chartered Company's administration of Rhodesia. 'The scrutiny may well have been disastrous for the Charter if the Select Committee had ever addressed itself to the task. In fact, it failed to do so . . .'* The Charter was saved and it was saved again in a parliamentary debate in July, in which Chamberlain championed Rhodes.

Rhodes declined to issue a writ against Olive Schreiner, because, it is said, of his admiration for her. Thus no ordinary court examined the matter.

That the book was 'horrible invention' was nowhere more violently asserted than in a literary curiosity. *Trooper Peter Halket* has a *doppelganger.* The Princess Catherine Radziwill published in 1900 *The Resurrection of Peter*, 'A Reply to Olive Schreiner'. She was a woman of talent and great audacity whose intrusion into his life Rhodes was to regret, not least when later she forged letters from him and promissory notes bearing his signature. Her Trooper Peter is resurrected temporarily in the African veld; once more the stars are shining as he sits at his little fire. (The style, even the phrasing, often echoes Olive's.) To him a luminous Stranger comes. It is Christ who bids him beware of false prophets. 'Beware of those hypo-

*Lockhart, J. G. and Woodhouse, the Hon. C. M., *Rhodes*, London, Hodder and Stoughton, 1963, p. 381

21

crites who preach good in order to beget evil; beware of the spirit of envy and malice . . .' There is much more in this vein, the dignified utterances becoming vituperative; sordid if somewhat obscure motives are attributed to Olive. But Rhodes, the Stranger says, 'works for me . . . he is a Creator who has sacrificed himself for the honour of the old flag.' The Stranger goes, and Peter, dying, is accepted into Heaven.

Lockhart and Woodhouse believe that *Trooper Peter Halket* gives a 'harsh but not unfounded' picture of the Company's men; '(they) were typical of a pioneering phase in their attitude to Africans'. There is general agreement that rape of black women and girls by whites and African police employed by whites was common. The system of forced labour was known about and frequently condemned in Britain. But this is no place for the sifting of evidence. There is no doubt that atrocities were committed on both sides.

Comment is required, however, on the photograph which appeared as frontispiece to the first edition, and on Trooper Peter's description (pp. 48-49) of the event whose outcome the photograph recorded. For if the description is invention, we cannot but be alienated. Peter speaks of there being one event and of the men as 'spies'. Olive Schreiner pointed out the tree to her family on a visit to

Bulawayo in 1911: her niece speaks of it as the tree on which the Matabele 'chiefs' were hanged; we do not know if 'chiefs' was the word Olive used on that occasion. No historical account I have seen mentions an episode in which chiefs or spies were hanged in this campaign in the manner Peter describes. The letterpress, says the *Manchester Guardian* of June 30, 1897, was supplied by a man called Sykes, serving with Colonel Plumer's volunteers in the Matabeleland Relief Force, whose book, *With Plumer in Matabeleland* the newspaper reviews.

The facts were perhaps worse than Olive knew. Here is Sykes's account of some activities of the garrison which relieved Bulawayo:

After a while it was a common occurrence for a detachment of troopers to go out in the early morning, shoot down some rebels, and return to breakfast.

What rebel spies were caught were summarily tried and hanged. There is a tree, known as the hanging tree, to the north of the town which did service as gallows. Hither the doomed men were conveyed. On the ropes being fastened to their necks, they were made to climb along an overhanging branch, and thence were pushed or compelled to jump into space after "a last look at Bulawayo". Their bodies were left suspended for twenty-four hours. This adoption of "lynch law" may not commend itself to the ultrahumane ideas associated with Exeter Hall, but it must be borne in mind that swift and decisive punishment was the only way to overawe the rebels, and actions which under other conditions might be regarded as brutal were justifiable – nay, absolutely essential – at such times as these.

Sykes was a fairminded, articulate man. He admired Rhodes, often showed sympathy with the Matabele, meticulously chronicled every aspect of the campaign. In his preface, he says he will present the less attractive side of campaigning; this may point a moral to 'civilians seized with military ardour'. Rhodes is not implicated in these hangings: Plumer was an Imperial officer.

The archives of T. Fisher Unwin have been destroyed: we do not know how Olive got the photograph, although there was a photographic detachment with Plumer's volunteers. We do not know why the photograph was suppressed: certainly there was an outcry of 'bad taste', as 'A.T.Q.C.' records.

* * *

'WE heard this morning that Cecil Rhodes died the day before yesterday. It was a greater shock to me than I could have believed possible . . . When death comes one forgets all the faults of a life and remembers only the awful tragedy of

24

the individual Soul – a great "might have been",' Olive wrote to a friend in 1902. In 1911, she made the long climb to Rhodes's grave and stood looking at it in silence.

*   *   *

THERE are weaknesses in *Trooper Peter Halket*. One would, I think, wish away, for example, the tedious sanctimony of the Cape preacher. But it is right that a book which Olive Schreiner herself valued should once more be made available to the public. To adapt her phrase: without the trumpet, we cannot hear the call.

MARION FRIEDMANN, London 1974

I

IT was a dark night; a chill breath was coming from the east; not enough to disturb the blaze of Trooper Peter Halket's fire, yet enough to make it quiver. He sat alone beside it on the top of a kopje.[1]

All about was an impenetrable darkness; not a star was visible in the black curve over his head.

He had been travelling with a dozen men who were taking provisions of mealies and rice to the next camp. He had been sent out to act as scout along a low range of hills, and had lost his way. Since eight in the morning he had wandered among long grasses, and ironstone kopjes, and stunted bush, and had come upon no sign of human habitation, but the remains of a burnt kraal,[2] and a down-trampled and now uncultivated mealie field, where a month before the Chartered Company's forces had destroyed a native settlement.

Three times in the day it had appeared to him that he had returned to the very spot from which he had started; nor was it his wish to travel very far, for he knew his comrades would

come back to look for him, to the neighbour-
hood where he had last been seen, when it was
found at the evening camping ground that he
did not appear.

Trooper Peter Halket was very weary. He
had eaten nothing all day; and had touched
little of the contents of a small flask of Cape
brandy he carried in his breast pocket, not
knowing when it would again be replenished.

As night drew near he determined to make
his resting place on the top of one of the kopjes,
which stood somewhat alone and apart from
the others. He could not easily be approached
there, without his knowing it. He had not much
fear of the natives; their kraals had been destroyed and their granaries burnt for thirty
miles round, and they themselves had fled: but
he feared, somewhat, the lions, which he had
never seen, but of which he had heard, and
which might be cowering in the long grasses and
brushwood at the kopje's foot: – and he feared,
vaguely, he hardly knew what, when he looked
forward to his first long night alone in the
veld.[3]

By the time the sun had set he had gathered
a little pile of stumps and branches on the top of
the kopje. He intended to keep a fire burning
all night; and as the darkness began to settle
down he lit it. It might be his friends would see
it from far, and come for him early in the
morning; and wild beasts would hardly ap-

proach him while he knelt beside it; and of the natives he felt there was little fear.

He built up the fire; and determined if it were possible to keep awake the whole night beside it.

He was a slight man of middle height, with a sloping forehead and pale blue eyes: but the jaws were hard set, and the thin lips of the large mouth were those of a man who could strongly desire the material good of life, and enjoy it when it came his way. Over the lower half of the face were scattered a few soft white hairs, the growth of early manhood.

From time to time he listened intently for possible sounds from the distance where his friends might be encamped, and might fire off their guns at seeing his light; or he listened yet more intently for sounds nearer at hand: but all was still, except for the occasional cracking of the wood in his own fire, and the slight whistle of the breeze as it crept past the stones on the kopje. He doubled up his great hat and put it in the pocket of his overcoat; and put on a little two-pointed cap his mother had made for him, which fitted so close that only one lock of white hair hung out over his forehead. He turned up the collar of his coat to shield his neck and ears, and threw it open in front that the blaze of the fire might warm him. He had known many nights colder than this when he had sat around the camp fire with his comrades, talking of the niggers they had shot or the kraals they had destroyed, or grumbling over their rations; but to-night the chill seemed to creep into his very bones.

The darkness of the night above him, and the silence of the veld about him, oppressed him. At times he even wished he might hear the cry of a jackal or of some larger beast of prey in the distance; and he wished that the wind would blow a little louder, instead of making that little wheezing sound as it passed the corners of the stones. He looked down at his gun which lay cocked ready on the ground at his right side; and from time to time he raised his hand automatically and fingered the cartridges in his belt. Then he stretched out his small wiry hands to the fire and warmed them. It was only half past ten, and it seemed to him he had been sitting here ten hours at the least.

After a while he threw two more large logs on the fire, and took the flask out of his pocket. He examined it carefully by the firelight to see how much it held: then he took a small draught, and examined it again to see how much it had fallen; and put it back in his breast pocket.

Then Trooper Peter Halket fell to thinking.

It was not often that he thought. On patrol and sitting round camp fires with the other men about him there was no time for it; and Peter Halket had never been given to much thinking. He had been a careless boy at the village school; and though, when he left, his mother paid the village apothecary to read learned books with him at night on history and science, he had not retained much of them. As a rule he lived in the world immediately about him, and let the things of the moment impinge on him, and fall off again as they would, without much reflection. But to-night on the kopje he fell to thinking, and his thoughts shaped themselves into connected chains.

He wondered first whether his mother would ever get the letter he had posted the week before, and whether it would be brought to her cottage or she would go to the post office to fetch it. And then, he fell to thinking of the little English village where he had been born, and where he had grown up. He saw his mother's fat white ducklings creep in and out under the gate, and waddle down to the little pond at the back of the yard; he saw the school house that he had hated so much as a boy, and from which he had so often run away to go a-fishing, or a-bird's-nesting. He saw the prints on the school house wall on which the afternoon sun used to shine when he was kept in; Jesus of Judea blessing the children, and one picture just over the door where he hung with his arms stretched out and the blood dropping from his feet. Then Peter Halket thought of the tower at the ruins which he had climbed so often for birds' eggs; and he saw his mother standing at her cottage gate when he came home in the evening, and he felt her arms round his neck as she kissed him; but he felt her tears on his cheek, because he had run away from school all day; and he seemed to be making apologies to her, and promising he never would do it again if only she would not cry. He had often thought of her since he left her, on board ship, and when he was working with the prospectors, and since he had joined the troop; but it had been in a vague way; he had not distinctly seen and felt her. But to-night he wished for her as he used to when he was a small boy and lay in his bed in the next room, and saw her shadow through the door as she bent over her wash-tub earning the money which was to feed and clothe him. He remembered how he called her and she came and tucked him in and called him 'Little Simon', which was his second name and had been his father's, and which she only called him when he was in bed at night, or when he was hurt.

He sat there staring into the blaze. He resolved he would make a great deal of money, and she should live with him. He would build a large house in the West End of London, the biggest that had ever been seen, and another in the country, and they should never work any more.

Peter Halket sat as one turned into stone, staring into the fire.

All men made money when they came to South Africa, – Barney Barnato, Rhodes – they all made money out of the country, eight millions, twelve millions, twenty-six millions, forty millions; why should not he!

Peter Halket started suddenly and listened. But it was only the wind coming up the kopje like a great wheezy beast creeping upwards; and he looked back into the fire.

He considered his business prospects. When he had served his time as volunteer he would have a large piece of land given him, and the Mashonas and Matabeles would have all their land taken away from them in time, and the Chartered Company would pass a law that they had to work for the white men; and he, Peter Halket, would make them work for him. He would make money.

Then he reflected on what he should do with the land if it were no good and he could not make anything out of it. Then, he should have to start a syndicate; called the Peter Halket Gold, or the Peter Halket Iron-mining, or some such name, Syndicate. Peter Halket was not very clear as to how it ought to be started; but he felt certain that he and some other men would have to take shares. They would not have to pay for them. And then they would get some big man in London to take shares. He need not pay for them; they would give them to him; and then the company would be floated. No one would have to pay anything; it was just the name – 'The Peter Halket Gold Mining Company, Limited'. It would float in London; and people there who didn't know the country would buy the shares; *they* would have to give ready money for them, of course; perhaps fifteen pounds a share when they were up! – Peter Halket's eyes blinked as he looked into the fire. – And then, when the market was up, he, Peter Halket, would sell out all his shares. If he gave himself only six thousand and sold them each for ten pounds, then he, Peter Halket, would have sixty thousand pounds! And then he would start another company, and another.

Peter Halket struck his knee softly with his hand.

That was the great thing – 'Always sell out at the right time.' That point Peter Halket was very clear on. He had heard it so often discussed. Give some shares to men with big names, and sell out: they can sell out too at the right time.

Peter Halket stroked his knee thoughtfully.

And then the other people, that bought the shares for cash! Well, they could sell out too; they could *all* sell out!

Then Peter Halket's mind got a little hazy. The matter was getting too difficult for him, like a rule of three sum at school when he could not see the relation between the two first terms and the third. Well, if they didn't like to sell out at the right time, it was their own faults. Why didn't they? He, Peter Halket, did not feel responsible for them. Everyone knew that you had to sell out at the right time. If they didn't choose to sell out at the right time, well, they didn't. '*It's the shares that you sell, not the shares you keep, that make the money.*'

But if they *couldn't* sell them?

Here Peter Halket hesitated. – Well, the British Government would have to buy them, if they were so bad no one else would; and then no one would lose. 'The British Government can't let British shareholders suffer.' He'd heard that often enough. The British taxpayer would have to pay for the Chartered Company, for the soldiers, and all the other things, if *it* couldn't, and take over the shares if it went smash, because there were lords and dukes and princes connected with it. And why shouldn't they pay for *his* company? He would have a lord in it too!

Peter Halket looked into the fire completely absorbed in his calculations. – Peter Halket, Esq., Director of the Peter Halket Gold Mining Company, Limited. Then, when he had got thousands, Peter Halket, Esq., M.P. Then, when he had millions, Sir Peter Halket, Privy Councillor!

He reflected deeply, looking into the blaze. If you had five or six millions you could go where you liked and do what you liked. You could go to Sandringham. You could marry anyone. No one would ask what your mother had been; it wouldn't matter.

A curious dull sinking sensation came over Peter Halket; and he drew in his broad leathern belt two holes tighter.

Even if you had only two millions you could have a cook and a valet, to go with you when you went into the veld or to the wars; and you could have as much champagne and other things as you liked. At that moment that seemed to Peter more important than going to Sandringham.

He took out his flask of Cape Smoke,[4] and drew a tiny draught from it.

Other men had come to South Africa with nothing, and had made everything! Why should not he?

He stuck small branches under the two great logs, and a glorious flame burst out. Then he listened again intently. The wind was falling and the night was becoming very still. It was a quarter to twelve now. His back ached, and he would have liked to lie down; but he dared not, for fear he should drop asleep. He leaned forward with his hands between his crossed knees, and watched the blaze he had made.

Then, after a while, Peter Halket's thoughts became less clear: they became at last, rather, a chain of disconnected pictures, painting themselves in irrelevant order on his brain, than a line of connected ideas. Now, as he looked into the crackling blaze, it seemed to be one of the fires they had made to burn the natives' grain by, and they were throwing in all they could not carry away: then, he seemed to see his mother's fat ducks waddling down the little path with the green grass on each side. Then, he seemed to see his huts where he lived with the prospectors, and the native women who used to live with him; and he wondered where the women were. Then – he saw the skull of an old Mashona blown off at the top, the hands still moving. He heard the loud cry of the native women and children as they turned the maxims on to the kraal; and then he heard the dynamite explode that blew up a cave. Then again he was working a maxim gun, but it seemed to him it was more like the reaping machine he used to work in England, and that what was going down before it was not yellow corn, but black men's heads; and he thought when he looked back they lay behind him in rows, like the corn in sheaves.

The logs sent up a flame clear and high, and, where they split, showed a burning core inside: the cracking and spluttering sounded in his brain like the discharge of a battery of artillery. Then he thought suddenly of a black woman he and another man caught alone in the bush, her baby on her back, but young and pretty. Well, they didn't shoot her! – and a black woman wasn't white! His mother didn't understand these things; it was all so different in England from South Africa. You couldn't be expected to do the same sort of things here as there. He had an unpleasant feeling that he was justifying himself to his mother, and that he didn't know how to.

He leaned further and further forward: so far at last, that the little white lock of his hair which hung out under his cap was almost singed by the fire. His eyes were still open, but the lids drooped over them, and his hands hung lower and lower between his knees. There was no picture left on his brain now, but simply an impress of the blazing logs before him.

Then, Trooper Peter Halket started. He sat up and listened. The wind had gone; there was not a sound: but he listened intently. The fire burnt up into the still air, two clear red tongues of flame.

Then, on the other side of the kopje he heard the sound of footsteps ascending; the slow even tread of bare feet coming up.

The hair on Trooper Peter Halket's forehead slowly stiffened itself. He had no thought of escaping; he was paralyzed with dread. He took up his gun. A deadly coldness crept from his feet to his head. He had worked a maxim gun in a fight when some hundred natives fell and only one white man had been wounded; and he had never known fear; but to-night his fingers were stiff on the lock of his gun. He knelt low, tending a little to one side of the fire, with his gun ready. A stone half sheltered him from anyone coming up from the other side of the kopje, and the instant the figure appeared over the edge he intended to fire.

Then, the thought flashed on him; what, and if it were one of his own comrades come in search of him, and no bare-footed enemy! The anguish of suspense wrung his heart; for an instant he hesitated. Then, in a cold agony of terror, he cried out, 'Who is there?'

And a voice replied in clear, slow English, 'A friend.'

Peter Halket almost let his gun drop, in the revulsion of feeling. The cold sweat which anguish had restrained burst out in large drops on his forehead; but he still knelt holding his gun.

'What do you want?' he cried out quiveringly.

From the darkness at the edge of the kopje a figure stepped out into the full blaze of the fire-light.

Trooper Peter Halket looked up at it.

It was the tall figure of a man, clad in one loose linen garment, reaching lower than his knees, and which clung close about him. His head, arms, and feet were bare. He carried no weapon of any kind; and on his shoulders hung heavy locks of dark hair.

Peter Halket looked up at him with astonishment. 'Are you alone?' he asked.

'Yes, I am alone.'

Peter Halket lowered his gun and knelt up.

'Lost your way, I suppose?' he said, still holding his weapon loosely.

'No; I have come to ask whether I may sit beside your fire for a while.'

'Certainly, certainly!' said Peter, eyeing the stranger's dress carefully, still holding his gun, but with the hand off the lock. 'I'm confoundedly glad of any company. It's a beastly night for anyone to be out alone. Wonder you find your way. Sit down! sit down!' Peter looked intently at the stranger; then he put his gun down at his side.

The stranger sat down on the opposite side of the fire. His complexion was dark; his arms and feet were bronzed; but his aquiline features, and the domed forehead, were not of any South African race.

'One of the Soudanese Rhodes brought with him from the north, I suppose?' said Peter, still eyeing him curiously.

'No; Cecil Rhodes has had nothing to do with my coming here,' said the stranger.

'Oh –' said Peter. 'You didn't perhaps happen to come across a company of men to-day, twelve white men and seven coloured, with three cart loads of provisions? We were taking them to the big camp, and I got parted from my troop this morning. I've not been able to find them, though I've been seeking for them ever since.'

The stranger warmed his hands slowly at the fire; then he raised his head: – 'They are camped at the foot of those hills to-night,' he said, pointing with his hand into the darkness at the left. 'To-morrow early they will be here, before the sun has risen.'

'Oh, you've met them, have you!' said Peter joyfully; 'that's why you weren't surprised at finding me here. Take a drop!' He took the small flask from his pocket and held it out. 'I'm sorry there's so little, but a drop will keep the cold out.'

The stranger bowed his head; but thanked and declined.

Peter raised the flask to his lips and took a small draught; then returned it to his pocket. The stranger folded his arms about his knees, and looked into the fire.

'Are you a Jew?' asked Peter, suddenly; as the firelight fell full on the stranger's face.

'Yes; I am a Jew.'

'Ah,' said Peter, 'that's why I wasn't able to make out at first what nation you could be of; your dress, you know –' Then he stopped, and said, 'Trading here, I suppose? Which country do you come from; are you a Spanish Jew?'

'I am a Jew of Palestine.'

'Ah!' said Peter; 'I haven't seen many from

that part yet. I came out with a lot on board ship; and I've seen Barnato and Beit; but they're not very much like you. I suppose it's coming from Palestine makes the difference.'

All fear of the stranger had now left Peter Halket. 'Come a little nearer the fire,' he said, 'you must be cold, you haven't too much wraps. I'm chill in this big coat.' Peter Halket pushed his gun a little further away from him; and threw another large log on the fire. 'I'm sorry I haven't anything to eat to offer you; but I haven't had anything myself since last night. It's beastly sickening, being out like this with nothing to eat. Wouldn't have thought a fellow-'d feel so bad after only a day of it. Have you ever been out without grub?' said Peter cheerfully, warming his hands at the blaze.

'Forty days and nights,' said the stranger.

'Forty days! Phe–e–w!' said Peter. 'You must have had a lot to drink, or you wouldn't have stood it. I was feeling blue enough when you turned up, but I'm better now, warmer.'

Peter Halket re-arranged the logs on the fire.

'In the employ of the Chartered Company, I suppose?' said Peter, looking into the fire he had made.

'No,' said the stranger; 'I have nothing to do with the Chartered Company.'

'Oh,' said Peter, 'I don't wonder, then, that things aren't looking very smart with you!

There's not too much cakes and ale up here for those that do belong to it, if they're not big-wigs, and none at all for those who don't. I tried it when I first came up here. I was with a prospector who was hooked on to the Company somehow, but I worked on my own account for the prospector by the day. I tell you what, it's not the men who work up here who make the money; it's the big-wigs who get the concessions!'

Peter felt exhilarated by the presence of the stranger. That one unarmed man had robbed him of all fear.

Seeing that the stranger did not take up the thread of conversation, he went on after a time: 'It wasn't such a bad life, though. I only wish I was back there again. I had two huts to my-self, and a couple of nigger girls. It's better fun,' said Peter, after a while, 'having these black women than whites. The whites you've got to support, but the niggers support you! And when you've done with them you can just get rid of them. I'm all for the nigger gals.' Peter laughed. But the stranger sat motionless with his arms about his knees.

'You got any girls?' said Peter. 'Care for niggers?'

'I love *all* women,' said the stranger, refolding his arms about his knees.

'Oh, you do, do you?' said Peter. 'Well, I'm pretty sick of them. I had bother enough with mine,' he said genially, warming his hands by the fire, and then interlocking the fingers and turning the palms towards the blaze as one who prepares to enjoy a good talk. 'One girl was only fifteen; I got her cheap from a policeman who was living with her, and she wasn't much. But the other, by gad! I never saw another nigger like her; well set up, I tell you, and as straight as that –' said Peter, holding up his finger in the firelight. 'She was thirty if she was a day. Fellows don't generally fancy women that age; they like slips of girls. But I set my heart on her the day I saw her. She belonged to the chap I was with. He got her up north. There was a devil of a row about his getting her, too; she'd got a nigger husband and two children; didn't want to leave them, or some nonsense of that sort: you know what these niggers are? Well, I tried to get the other fellow to let me have her, but the devil a bit he would. I'd only got the other girls, and I didn't much fancy her; she was only a child. Well, I went down Umtali way and got a lot of liquor and stuff, and when I got back to camp I found them clean dried out. They hadn't had a drop of liquor in camp for ten days, and the rainy season coming on and no knowing when they'd get any. Well, I'd a 'vatje' of Old Dop[5] as high as that –,' indicating with his hand an object about two feet high, 'and the other fellow wanted to buy it from me. I knew two of that. I

43

said I wanted it for myself. He offered me this, and he offered me that. At last I said, 'Well, just to oblige you, I give you the 'vatje' and you give me the girl!' And so he did. Most people wouldn't have fancied a nigger girl who'd had two nigger children, but I didn't mind; it's all the same to me. And I tell you she worked. She made a garden, and she and the other girl worked in it; I tell you I didn't need to buy a sixpence of food for them in six months, and I used to sell green mealies and pumpkins to all the fellows about. There weren't many flies on her, I tell you. She picked up English quicker than I picked up her lingo, and took to wearing a dress and shawl.'

The stranger still sat motionless, looking into the fire.

Peter Halket reseated himself more comfortably before the fire. 'Well, I came home to the huts one day, rather suddenly, you know, to fetch something; and what did I find? She, talking at the hut door with a nigger man. Now it was my strict orders they were neither to speak a word to a nigger man at all; so I asked what it was. And she answers, as cool as can be, that he was a stranger going past on the road, and asked her to give him a drink of water. Well, I just ordered him off. I didn't think anything more about it. But I remember now. I saw him hanging about the camp the day after. Well, she came to me the next day and asked

44

me for a lot of cartridges. She'd never asked me for anything before. I asked her what the devil a woman wanted with cartridges, and she said the old nigger woman who helped carry in water to the garden said she couldn't stay and help her any more unless she got some cartridges to give her son who was going up north hunting elephants. The woman got over me to give her the cartridges because she was going to have a kid, and she said she couldn't do the watering without help. So I gave them her. I never put two and two together.'

'Well, when I heard that the Company was going to have a row with the Matabele, I thought I'd volunteer. They said there was lots of loot to be got, and land to be given out, and that sort of thing, and I thought I'd only be gone about three months. So I went. I left those women there, and a lot of stuff in the garden and some sugar and rice, and I told them not to leave till I came back; and I asked the other man to keep an eye on them. Both those women were Mashonas. They always said the Mashonas didn't love the Matabele; but, by God, it turned out that they loved them better than they loved us. They've got the damned impertinence to say, that the Matabele oppressed them sometimes, but the white man oppresses them all the time!'

'Well, I left those women there,' said Peter, dropping his hands on his knees. 'Mind you,

I'd treated those women really well. I'd never given either of them one touch all the time I had them. I was the talk of all the fellows round, the way I treated them. Well, I hadn't been gone a month, when I got a letter from the man I worked with, the one who had the woman first – he's dead now, poor fellow; they found him at his hut door with his throat cut – and what do you think he said to me? Why, I hadn't been gone six hours when those two women skooted! It was all the big one. What do you think she did? She took every ounce of ball and cartridge she could find in that hut, and my old Martini-Henry, and even the lid off the tea-box to melt into bullets for the old muzzle-loaders they have; and off she went, and took the young one too. The fellow wrote me they didn't touch another thing: they left the shawls and dresses I gave them kicking about the huts, and went off naked with only their blankets and the ammunition on their heads. A nigger man met them twenty miles off, and he said they were skooting up for Lo Magundis country as fast as they could go.'

'And do you know,' said Peter, striking his knee, and looking impressively across the fire at the stranger; 'what I'm as sure of as that I'm sitting here? It's that nigger I caught at my hut, that day, was her nigger husband! He'd come to fetch her that time; and when she saw she couldn't get away without our catching her, she got the cartridges for *him!*' Peter paused impressively between the words. 'And now she's gone back to him. It's for him she's taken that ammunition!'

Peter looked across the fire at the stranger, to see what impression his story was making.

'I tell you what,' said Peter, 'if I'd had any idea that day who that bloody nigger was, the day I saw him standing at my door, I'd have given him one cartridge in the back of his head more than ever he reckoned for!' Peter looked triumphantly at the stranger. This was his only story; and he had told it a score of times round the camp fire for the benefit of some new-comer. When this point was reached, a low murmur of applause and sympathy always ran round the group: tonight there was quiet; the stranger's large dark eyes watched the fire almost as though he heard nothing.

'I shouldn't have minded so much,' said Peter after a while, 'though no man likes to have his woman taken away from him; but she was going to have a kid in a month or two – and so was the little one for anything I know; she looked like it! I expect they did away with it before it came; they've no hearts, these niggers; they'd think nothing of doing that with a white man's child. They've no hearts; they'd rather go back to a black man, however well you've treated them. It's all right if you get them quite young and keep them away from their own people; but if once a nigger woman's had a nigger man and had children by him, you might as well try to hold a she-devil! they'll always go back. If ever I'm shot, it's as likely as not it'll be by my own gun, with my own cartridges. And she'd stand by and watch it, and cheer them on; though I never gave her a blow all the time she was with me. But I tell you what – if ever I come across that bloody nigger, I'll take it out of him. He won't count many days to his year, after I've spotted him!' Peter Halket paused. It seemed to him that the eyes under their heavy, curled lashes, were looking at something beyond him with an infinite sadness, almost as of eyes that wept.

'You look awfully tired,' said Peter; 'wouldn't you like to lie down and sleep? You could put your head down on that stone, and I'd keep watch.'

'I have no need of sleep,' the stranger said; 'I will watch with you.'

'You've been in the wars, too, I see,' said Peter, bending forward a little, and looking at the stranger's feet. 'By God! Both of them! – And right through! You must had a bad time of it?'

'It was very long ago,' said the stranger.

Peter Halket threw two more logs on the fire. 'Do you know,' he said, 'I've been wondering ever since you came, who it was you reminded me of. It's my mother! You're not like her in the face, but when your eyes look at me it seems to me as if it was she looking at me. Curious, isn't it? I don't know you from Adam, and you've hardly spoken a word since you came; and yet I seem as if I'd known you all my life.' Peter moved a little nearer him. 'I was awfully afraid of you when you first came; even when I first saw you; – you aren't dressed as most of us dress, you know. But the minute the fire shone on your face I said, "It's all right." Curious, isn't it?' said Peter. 'I don't know you from Adam, but if you were to take up my gun and point it at me, I wouldn't move! I'd lie down here and go to sleep with my head at your feet; curious, isn't it, when I don't know you from Adam? My name's Peter Halket. What's yours?'

But the stranger was arranging the logs on the fire. The flames shot up bright and high, and almost hid him from Peter Halket's view.

'By gad! how they burn when you arrange them!' said Peter.

They sat quiet in the blaze for a while.

Then Peter said, 'Did you see any niggers about yesterday? I haven't come across any in this part.'

'There is,' said the stranger, raising himself, 'an old woman in a cave over yonder, and there is one man in the bush, ten miles from this spot. He has lived there six weeks, since you destroyed the kraal, living on roots or herbs. He

4

was wounded in the thigh, and left for dead. He is waiting till you have all left this part of the country that he may set out to follow his own people. His leg is not yet so strong that he may walk fast.'

'Did you speak to him?' said Peter.

'I took him down to the water where a large pool was. The bank was too high for the man to descend alone.'

'It's a lucky thing for you our fellows didn't catch you,' said Peter. 'Our captain's a regular little martinet. He'd shoot you as soon as look at you, if he saw you fooling round with a wounded nigger. It's lucky you kept out of his way.'

'The young ravens have meat given to them,' said the stranger, lifting himself up; 'and the lions go down to the streams to drink.'

'Ah – yes –' said Peter; 'but that's because we can't help it!'

They were silent again for a little while. Then Peter, seeing that the stranger showed no inclination to speak, said, 'Did you hear of the spree they had up Bulawayo way, hanging those three niggers for spies? I wasn't there myself, but a fellow who was told me they made the niggers jump down from the tree and hang themselves; one fellow wouldn't bally jump, till they gave him a charge of buckshot in the back: and then he caught hold of a branch with his hands and they had to shoot 'em loose.

He didn't like hanging. I don't know if it's true, of course; I wasn't there myself, but a fellow who was told me. Another fellow who was at Bulawayo, but who wasn't there when they were hung, said they fired at them just after they jumped, to kill 'em. I –'

'I was there,' said the stranger.

'Oh, you were?' said Peter. 'I saw a photograph of the niggers hanging, and our fellows standing round smoking; but I didn't see you in it. I suppose you'd just gone away?'

'I was beside the men when they were hung,' said the stranger.

'Oh, you were, were you?' said Peter. 'I don't much care about seeing that sort of thing myself. Some fellows think it's the best fun out to see the niggers kick; but I can't stand it: it turns my stomach. It's not liver-heartedness,' said Peter, quickly, anxious to remove any adverse impression as to his courage which the stranger might form; 'if it's shooting or fighting, I'm there. I've potted as many niggers as any man in our troop, I bet. It's floggings and hangings I'm off. It's the way one's brought up, you know. My mother never even would kill our ducks; she let them die of old age, and we had the feathers and the eggs: and she was always drumming into me; – don't hit a fellow smaller than yourself; don't hit a fellow weaker than yourself; don't hit a fellow unless he can hit you back as good again. When you've always had that sort of thing drummed into you, you can't get rid of it, somehow. Now there was that other nigger they shot. They say he sat as still as if he was cut out of stone, with his arms round his legs; and some of the fellows gave him blows about the head and face before they took him off to shoot him. Now, that's the sort of thing I can't do. It makes me sick here, somehow.' Peter put his hand rather low down over the pit of his stomach. 'I'll shoot as many as you like if they'll run, but they mustn't be tied up.'

'I was there when that man was shot,' said the stranger.

'Why, you seem to have been everywhere,' said Peter. 'Have you seen Cecil Rhodes?'

'Yes, I have seen him,' said the stranger.

'Now *he's* death on niggers,' said Peter Halket, warming his hands by the fire; 'they say when he was Prime Minister down in the Colony he tried to pass a law that would give masters and mistresses the right to have their servants flogged whenever they did anything they didn't like; but the other Englishmen wouldn't let him pass it. But *here* he can do what he likes. That's the reason some fellows don't want him to be sent away. They say, "If we get the British Government here, they'll be giving the niggers land to live on; and let them have the vote, and get civilised and educated, and all that sort of thing; but Cecil Rhodes, he'll keep their noses to the grindstone." *I prefer land to niggers*, he says. They say he's going to parcel them out, and make them work on our lands whether they like it or not – just as good as having slaves, you know: and you haven't the bother of looking after them when they're old. Now, there I'm with Rhodes; I think it's an awfully good move. We don't come out here to work; it's all very well in England; but we've come here to make money, and how are we to make it, unless you get niggers to work for you, or start a syndicate? He's death on niggers, is Rhodes!' said Peter, meditating; 'they say if we had the British Government here and you were thrashing a nigger and something happened, there'd be an investigation, and all that sort of thing. But, with Cecil, it's all right, you can do what you like with the niggers, provided you don't get *him* into trouble.'

The stranger watched the clear flame as it burnt up high in the still night air; then suddenly he started.

'What is it?' said Peter; 'do you hear anything?'

'I hear far off,' said the stranger, 'the sound of weeping, and the sound of blows. And I hear the voices of men and women calling to me.'

Peter listened intently. 'I don't hear anything!' he said. 'It must be in your head. I sometimes get a noise in mine.' He listened intently. 'No, there's nothing. It's all so deadly still.'

They sat silent for a while.

'Peter Simon Halket,' said the stranger suddenly – Peter started; he had not told him his second name – 'if it should come to pass that you should obtain those lands you have desired, and you should obtain black men to labour on them and make to yourself great wealth; or should you create that company' – Peter started – 'and fools should buy from you, so that you became the richest man in the land; and if you should take to yourself wide lands, and raise to yourself great palaces, so that princes and great men of earth crept up to you and laid their hands against yours, so that you might slip gold into them – what would it profit you?'

'Profit!' Peter Halket stared: 'Why, it would profit everything. What makes Beit and Rhodes and Barnato so great? If you've got eight millions –'

'Peter Simon Halket, which of those souls you have seen on earth is to you greatest?' said the stranger, 'Which soul is to you fairest?'

'Ah,' said Peter, 'but we weren't talking of souls at all; we were talking of money. Of course if it comes to souls, my mother's the best person I've ever seen. But what does it help her? She's got to stand washing clothes for those stuck-up nincompoops of fine ladies! Wait till I've got money! It'll be somebody else then, who –'

'Peter Halket,' said the stranger, 'who is the greatest; he who serves or he who is served?' Peter looked at the stranger: then it flashed on him that he was mad.

'Oh,' he said, 'if it comes to that, what's anything! You might as well say, sitting there in your old linen shirt, that you were as great as Rhodes or Beit or Barnato, or a king. Of course a man's just the same whatever he's got on or whatever he has; but he isn't the same to other people.'

'There have kings been born in stables,' said the stranger.

Then Peter saw that he was joking, and laughed. 'It must have been a long time ago; they don't get born there now,' he said. 'Why, if God Almighty came to this country, and hadn't half-a-million in shares, they wouldn't think much of Him.'

Peter built up his fire. Suddenly he felt the stranger's eyes were fixed on him.

'Who gave you your land?' the stranger asked.

'Mine! Why, the Chartered Company,' said Peter.

The stranger looked back into the fire. 'And who gave it to them?' he asked softly.

'Why, England, of course. She gave them the land to far beyond the Zambesi to do what they liked with, and make as much money out of as they could, and she'd back 'em.'

'Who gave the land to the men and women of England?' asked the stranger softly.

'Why, the devil! They said it was theirs, and of course it was,' said Peter.

'And the people of the land: did England give you the people also?'

Peter looked a little doubtfully at the stranger. 'Yes, of course, she gave us the people; what use would the land have been to us otherwise?'

'And who gave her the people, the living flesh and blood, that she might give them away, into the hands of others?' asked the stranger, raising himself.

Peter looked at him and was half afeared. 'Well, what could she do with a lot of miserable niggers, if she didn't give them to us? A lot of good-for-nothing rebels they are, too,' said Peter.

'What is a rebel?' asked the stranger.

'My Gawd!' said Peter, 'you must have lived out of the world if you don't know what a rebel is! A rebel is a man who fights against his king and his country. These bloody niggers here are rebels because they are fighting against us. They don't want the Chartered Company to have them. But they'll have to. We'll teach them a lesson,' said Peter Halket, the pugilistic spirit rising, firmly reseating himself on the South African earth, which two years before he had never heard of, and eighteen months before he had never seen, as if it had been his mother earth, and the land in which he first saw light.

The stranger watched the fire; then he said musingly, 'I have seen a land far from here. In that land are men of two kinds who live side by side. Well nigh a thousand years ago one conquered the other; they have lived together since. To-day the one people seeks to drive forth the other who conquered them. Are these men rebels, too?'

'Well,' said Peter, pleased at being deferred to, 'that all depends who they are, you know!'

'They call the one nation Turks, and the other Armenians,' said the stranger.

'Oh, the Armenians aren't rebels,' said Peter; 'they are on our side! The papers are all full of it,' said Peter, pleased to show his knowledge. 'Those bloody Turks! What right had they to conquer the Armenians? Who gave them their land? I'd like to have a shot at them myself!'

'*Why* are Armenians not rebels?' asked the stranger, gently.

'Oh, you do ask such curious questions,' said Peter. 'If they don't like the Turks, why should they have 'em? If the French came now and conquered us, and we tried to drive them out first chance we had; you wouldn't call *us* rebels! Why shouldn't they try to turn those bloody Turks out? Besides,' said Peter, bending over and talking in the manner of one who imparts secret and important information; 'you see, if

57

we don't help the Armenians the Russians would; and we,' said Peter, looking exceedingly knowing, 'we've got to prevent that: they'd get the land; and it's on the road to India. And we don't mean them to. I suppose you don't know much about politics in Palestine?' said Peter, looking kindly and patronisingly at the stranger.

'If these men,' said the stranger, 'would rather be free, or be under the British Government, than under the Chartered Company, why, when they resist the Chartered Company, are they more rebels than the Armenians when they resist the Turk? Is the Chartered Company God, that every knee should bow before it, and before it every head be bent? Would you, the white men of England, submit to its rule for one day?'

'Ah,' said Peter, 'no, of course we shouldn't, but we are white men, and so are the Armenians – almost –' Then he glanced at the stranger's dark face, and added quickly, 'At least, it's not the colour that matters, you know. I rather like a dark face, my mother's eyes are brown – but the Armenians, you know, they've got long hair like us.'

'Oh, it is the hair, then, that matters,' said the stranger softly.

'Oh, well,' said Peter, 'it's not altogether, of course. But it's quite a different thing, the Armenians wanting to get rid of the Turks, and these bloody niggers wanting to get rid of the Chartered Company. Besides, the Armenians are Christians, like us!'

'Are *you* Christians?' A strange storm broke across the stranger's features; he rose to his feet.

'Why, of course, we are!' said Peter. 'We're all Christians, we English. Perhaps you don't like Christians, though? Some Jews don't, I know,' said Peter, looking up soothingly at him.

'I neither love nor hate any man for that which he is called,' said the stranger; 'the name boots nothing.'

The stranger sat down again beside the fire, and folded his hands.

'Is the Chartered Company Christian also?' he asked.

'Yes, oh yes,' said Peter.

'What is a Christian?' asked the stranger.

'Well, now, you really do ask such curious questions. A Christian is a man who believes in Heaven and Hell, and God and the Bible, and in Jesus Christ, that he'll save him from going to Hell, and if he believes he'll be saved, he *will* be saved.'

'But here, in this world, what is a Christian?'

'Why,' said Peter, 'I'm a Christian – we're all Christians.'

The stranger looked into the fire; and Peter thought he would change the subject. 'It's curious how like my mother you are; I mean, your ways. She was always saying to me, "Don't be too anxious to make money, Peter. Too much wealth is as bad as too much poverty." You're very like her.'

After a while Peter said, bending over a little towards the stranger, 'If you don't want to make money, what did you come to this land for? No one comes here for anything else. Are you in with the Portuguese?'

'I am not more with one people than with another,' said the stranger. 'The Frenchman is not more to me than the Englishman, the Englishman than the Kaffir, the Kaffir than the Chinaman. I have heard,' said the stranger, 'the black infant cry as it crept on its mother's body and sought for her breast as she lay dead in the roadway. I have heard also the rich man's child wail in the palace. I hear all cries.'

Peter looked intently at him. 'Why, who are you?' he said; then, bending nearer to the stranger and looking up, he added, 'What is it that you are doing here?'

'I belong,' said the stranger, 'to the strongest company on earth.'

'Oh,' said Peter, sitting up, the look of wonder passing from his face. 'So that's it, is it? Is it diamonds, or gold, or lands?'

'We are the most vast of all companies on the earth,' said the stranger; 'and we are always growing. We have among us men of every race and from every land; the Esquimo, the Chinaman, the Turk, and the Englishman, we have of them all. We have men of every religion, Buddhists, Mahomedans, Confucians, Freethinkers, Atheists, Christians, Jews. It matters to us nothing by what name the man is named, so he be one of us.'

And Peter said, 'It must be hard for you all to understand one another, if you are of so many different kinds?'

The stranger answered, 'There is a sign by which we all know one another, and by which all the world may know us.'[6]

And Peter said, 'What is that sign?'

But the stranger was silent.

'Oh, a kind of freemasonry!' said Peter, leaning on his elbow towards the stranger, and looking up at him from under his pointed cap.

'Are there any more of you here in this country?'

'There are,' said the stranger. Then he pointed with his hand into the darkness. 'There in a cave were two women. When you blew the cave up they were left unhurt behind a fallen rock. When you took away all the grain, and burnt what you could not carry, there was one basketful that you knew nothing of. The women stayed there, for one was eighty, and one near the time of her giving birth; and they dared not set out to follow the remnant of their tribe because you were in the plains below. Every day the old woman doled grain from the basket; and at night they cooked it in their cave where you could not see their smoke; and every day the old woman gave the young one two handfuls and kept one for herself, saying, "Because of the child within you." And when the child was born and the young woman strong, the old woman took a cloth and filled it with all the grain that was in the basket; and she put the grain on the young woman's head and tied the child on her back, and said, "Go, keeping always along the bank of the river, till you come north of the land where our people are gone; and some day you can send and fetch me." And the young woman said, "Have you corn in the basket to last till they come?" And she said, "I have enough." And she sat at the broken door of the cave and watched the young woman go down the hill and up the river bank till she was hidden by the bush; and she looked down at the plain below, and she saw the spot where the kraal had been and where she had planted mealies when she was a young girl –'

'I met a woman with corn on her head and a child on her back!' said Peter under his breath.

'– And to-night I saw her sit again at the door of the cave; and when the sun had set she grew cold; and she crept in and lay down by the basket. To-night, at half-past three, she will die. I have known her since she was a little child and played about the huts, while her mother worked in the mealie fields. She was one of our company.'

'Oh,' said Peter.

'Other members we have here,' said the stranger. 'There was a prospector' – he pointed north; 'he was a man who drank and swore when it listed him; but he had many servants, and they knew where to find him in need. When they were ill, he tended them with his own hands; when they were in trouble, they came to him for help. When this war began, and all black men's hearts were bitter, because certain white men had lied to them, and their envoys had been killed when they would have asked England to put her hand out over them; at that time certain of the men who fought the white men came to the prospector's hut. And the prospector fired at them from a hole he had cut in his door; but they fired back at him with an old elephant gun, and the bullet pierced his side and he fell on the floor: – because the innocent man suffers oftentimes for the guilty, and the merciful man falls while the oppressor flourishes. Then his black servant who was with him took him quickly in his arms, and carried him out at the back of the hut, and down into the river bed where the water flowed and no man could trace his footsteps, and hid him in a hole in the river wall. And when the men broke into the hut they could find no white man, and no traces of his feet. But at evening, when the black servant returned to the hut to get food and medicine for his master, the men who were fighting caught him, and they said, "Oh, you betrayer of your people, white man's dog, who are on the side of those who take our lands and our wives and our daughters before our eyes; tell us where you have hidden him?" And when he would not answer them, they killed him before the door of the hut. And when the night came, the white man crept up on his hands and knees, and came to his hut to look for food. All the other men were gone, but his servant lay dead before the door; and the white man knew how it must have happened. He could not creep further, and he lay down before the door, and that night the white man and the black lay there dead together, side by side. Both those men were of my friends.'

'It was damned plucky of the nigger,' said Peter; 'but I've heard of their doing that sort of thing before. Even of a girl who wouldn't tell where her mistress was, and getting killed. But,' he added doubtfully, 'all your company seem to be niggers or to get killed?'

'They are of all races,' said the stranger. 'In a city in the old Colony is one of us, small of stature and small of voice. It came to pass on a certain Sunday morning, when the men and women were gathered before him, that he mounted his pulpit: and he said when the time for the sermon came, "In place that I should speak to you, I will read you a history." And he opened an old book more than two thousand years old: and he read: "Now it came to pass that Naboth the Jezreelite had a vineyard, which was in Jezreel, hard by the palace of Ahab king of Samaria." '

' "And Ahab spake unto Naboth, saying, Give me thy vineyard, that I may have it for a garden of herbs, because it is near unto my house: and I will give thee for it a better vineyard than it; or, if it seemeth good to thee, I will give thee the worth of it in money." '

' "And Naboth said to Ahab, The Lord forbid it me, that I should give the inheritance of my father unto thee." '

' "And Ahab came into his house heavy and displeased because of the word which Naboth the Jezreelite had spoken unto him; for he had said, I will not give thee the inheritance of my fathers." '

'The man read the whole story until it was ended. Then he closed the book, and he said, "My friends, Naboth has a vineyard in this land; and in it there is much gold; and Ahab has desired to have it that the wealth may be his." '

'And he put the old book aside, and he took up another which was written yesterday. And the men and women whispered one to another, even in the church, "Is not that the Blue Book Report of the Select Committee of the Cape Parliament on the Jameson Raid?" '

'And the man said, "Friends, the first story I

have read you is one of the oldest stories of the world: the story I am about to read you is one of the newest. Truth is not more truth because it is three thousand years old, nor is it less truth because it is of yesterday. All books which throw light on truth are God's books, therefore I shall read to you from the pages before me. Shall the story of Ahab king of Samaria profit us when we know not the story of the Ahabs of our day; and the Naboths of our land be stoned while we sit at ease?" And he read to them portions of that book. And certain rich men and women rose up and went out even while he spoke, and his wife also went out.'

'And when the service was ended and the man returned to his home, his wife came to him weeping; and she said, "Did you see how some of the most wealthy and important people got up and went out this morning? Why did you preach such a sermon, when we were just going to have the new wing added to our house, and you thought they were going to raise your salary? You have not a single Boer in your congregation! Why need you say the Chartered Company raid on Johannesburg was wrong?" '

'He said, "My wife, if I believe that certain men whom we have raised on high, and to whom we have given power, have done a cowardly wrong, shall I not say it?" '

'And she said, "Yes, and only a little while ago, when Rhodes was licking the dust off the

Boers' feet that he might keep them from suspecting while he got ready this affair, then you attacked both Rhodes and the Bond[7] for trying to pass a Bill for flogging the niggers, and we lost fifty pounds we might have got for the church?" And he said, "My wife, cannot God be worshipped as well under the dome of the heaven He made as in a golden palace? Shall a man keep silence, when he sees oppression, to earn money for God? If I have defended the black man when I believed him to be wronged, shall I not also defend the white man, my flesh-brother? Shall we speak when one man is wronged and not when it is another?" '

'And she said, "Yes, but you have your family and yourself to think of! Why are you always in opposition to the people who could do something for us? You are only loved by the poor. If it is necessary for you to attack some one, why don't you attack the Jews for killing Christ, or Herod, or Pontius Pilate; why don't you leave alone the men who are in power to-day, and who with their money can crush you!" '

'And he said, "Oh my wife, those Jews, and Herod, and Pontius Pilate are long dead. If I should preach of them now, would it help them? Would it save one living thing from their clutches? The past is dead, it lives only for us to learn from. The present, the present only, is ours to work in, and the future ours to create. Is all the gold of Johannesburg or are all the diamonds in Kimberley worth, that one Christian man should fall by the hand of his fellows – aye, or one heathen brother?" '

'And she answered, "Oh, that is all very well. If you were a really eloquent preacher, and could draw hundreds of men about you, and in time form a great party with you at its head, I shouldn't mind what you said. But you, with your little figure and your little voice, who will ever follow you? You will be left all alone; that is all the good that will ever come to you through it." '

'And he said, "Oh my wife, have I not waited and watched and hoped that they who are nobler and stronger than I, all over this land, would lift up their voices and speak – and there is only a deadly silence? Here and there one has dared to speak aloud; but the rest whisper behind the hand; one says, "My son has a post, he would lose it if I spoke loud"; and another says, "I have a promise of land"; and another, "I am socially intimate with these men, and should lose my social standing if I let my voice be heard." Oh my wife, our land, our goodly land, which we had hoped would be free and strong among the peoples of earth, is rotten and honeycombed with the tyranny of gold! We who had hoped to stand first in the Anglo-Saxon sisterhood for justice and freedom, are not even fit to stand last. Do I not know only too bitterly how weak is my voice; and that that which I can do

68

is as nothing: but shall I remain silent? Shall the glow-worm refuse to give its light, because it is not a star set up on high; shall the broken stick refuse to burn and warm one frozen man's hands, because it is not a beacon-light flaming across the earth? Ever a voice is behind my shoulder, that whispers to me – "*Why break your head against a stone wall? Leave this work to the greater and larger men of your people; they who will do it better than you can do it! Why break your heart when life could be so fair to you?*" But, oh my wife, the strong men are silent! and shall I not speak, though I know my power is as nothing?" '

'He laid his head upon his hands.'

'And she said, "I cannot understand you. When I come home and tell you that this man drinks, or that that woman has got into trouble, you always answer me, "Wife, what business is it of ours if so be that we cannot help them?" A little innocent gossip offends you; and you go to visit people and treat them as your friends, into whose house I would not go. Yet when the richest and strongest men in the land, who could crush you with their money, as a boy crushes a fly between his finger and thumb, take a certain course, you stand and oppose them." '

'And he said, "My wife, with the sins of the private man, what have I to do, if so be I have not led him into them? Am I guilty? I have enough to do looking after my own sins. The sin that a man sins against himself is his alone, not mine; the sin that a man sins against his fellows is his and theirs, not mine: but the sins that a man sins, in that he is taken up by the hands of a people and set up on high, and whose hand they have armed with their sword, whose power to strike is their power – his sins are theirs; there is no man so small in the whole nation that he dares say, "I have no responsibility for this man's action." We armed him, we raised him, we strengthened him, and the evil he accomplishes is more ours than his. If this man's end in South Africa should be accomplished, and the day should come when, from the Zambesi to the sea, white man should fly at white man's throat, and every man's heart burn with bitterness against his fellow, and the land be bathed with blood as rain – shall I then dare to pray, who have now feared to speak? Do not think I wish for punishment upon these men. Let them take the millions they have wrung out of this land, and go to the lands of their birth, and live in wealth, luxury, and joy; but let them leave this land they have tortured and ruined. Let them keep the money they have made here; we may be the poorer for it; but they cannot then crush our freedom with it. Shall I ask my God Sunday by Sunday to brood across the land, and bind all its children's hearts in a close-knit fellowship; – yet, when I see its people betrayed, and their jawbone broken by a stroke from the hand of gold;

when I see freedom passing from us, and the whole land being grasped by the golden claw, so that the generation after us shall be born without freedom, to labour for the men who have grasped all, shall I hold my peace? The Boer and the Englishman who have been in this land, have not always loved mercy, nor have they always sought after justice; but the little finger of the speculator and monopolist who are devouring this land will be thicker on the backs of the children of this land, black and white, than the lions of the Dutchmen and Englishmen who have been." '

'And she said, "I have heard it said that it was our duty to sacrifice ourselves for the men and women living in the world at the same time as ourselves; but I never before heard that we had to sacrifice ourselves for people that are not born. What are they to you? You will be dust, and lying in your grave, before that time comes. If you believe in God," she said, "why cannot you leave it to Him to bring good out of all this evil? Does He need *you* to be made a martyr of? or will the world be lost without *you?*" '

'He said, "Wife, if my right hand be in a fire, shall I not pull it out? Shall I say, "God may bring good out of this evil," and let it burn? That Unknown that lies beyond us we know of no otherwise than through its manifestation in our own hearts; it works no otherwise upon the sons of men than through man. And shall I feel no bond binding me to the men to come, and desire no good or beauty for them – I, who am what I am, and enjoy what I enjoy, because for countless ages in the past men have lived and laboured, who lived not for themselves alone, and counted no costs? Would the great statue, the great poem, the great reform ever be accomplished, if men counted the cost and created for their own lives alone? And no man liveth to himself, and no man dieth to himself. You cannot tell me not to love the men who shall be after me; a soft voice within me, I know not what, cries out ever, "Live for them as for your own children." When in the circle of my own small life all is dark, and I despair, hope springs up in me when I remember that something nobler and fairer may spring up in the spot where I now stand." '

'And she said, "You want to put everyone against us! The other women will not call on me; and our church is more and more made up of poor people. Money holds by money. If your congregation were Dutchmen, I know you would be always preaching to love the Englishmen, and be kind to niggers. If they were Kaffirs you would always be telling them to help white men. You will never be on the side of the people who can do anything for us! You know the offer we had from –" '

'And he said, "Oh my wife, what are the

Boer, and the Russian, and the Turk to me; am I responsible for their action? It is my own nation, mine, which I love as a man loves his own soul, whose acts touch me. I would that wherever our flag was planted the feeble or oppressed peoples of earth might gather under it, saying, "Under this banner is freedom and justice which knows no race or colour." I wish that on our banner were blazoned in large letters *Justice and Mercy*, and that in every new land which our feet touch, every son among us might see ever blazoned above his head that banner, and below it the great order: – "*By this sign, Conquer!*" – and that the pirate flag which some men now wave in its place, may be torn down and furled for ever! Shall I condone the action of some, simply because they happen to be of my own race, when in Bushman or Hottentot I would condemn it? Shall men belonging to one of the mightiest races of earth, creep softly on their bellies, to attack an unwarned neighbour; when even the Kaffir has again and again given notice of war, saying, "Be ready, on such and such a day I come to fight you"? Is England's power so broken, and our race so enfeebled, that we dare no longer to proclaim war; but must creep silently upon our bellies in the dark to stab, like a subject people to whom no other course is open? These men are English; but not English-*men*. When the men of our race fight, they go to war with a blazoned flag and the loud trumpet before them. It is because I am an Englishman that these things crush me. Better that ten thousand of us should lie dead and defeated on one battlefield, fighting for some great cause, and my own sons among them, than that those twelve poor boys should have fallen at Doornkop, fighting to fill up the pockets of those already o'er-heavy with gold." '

'And she said, "*You*, what does it matter what you feel or think; *you* will never be able to do anything!" '

'And he said, "Oh my wife, stand by me; do not crush me. For me in this matter there is no path but one on which light shines." '

'And she said, "You are very unkind; you don't care what the people say about us!" and she wept bitterly, and went out of the room. But as soon as the door was shut, she dried her tears; and she said to herself, "Now he will never dare to preach such a sermon again. He dares never oppose me when once I have set down my foot." '

'And the man spoke to no one, and went out alone in the veld. All the afternoon he walked up and down among the sand and low bushes; and I walked there beside him.'

'And when the evening came, he went back to his chapel. Many were absent, but the elders sat in their places, and his wife also was there. And the light shone on the empty benches. And when the time came he opened the old book of

the Jews; and he turned the leaves and read: –
"If thou forbear to deliver them that are drawn
unto death, and those that are ready to be
slain; if thou sayest, "Behold we knew it not!"
Doth not he that pondereth the heart consider
it? and he that keepeth thy soul, doth he not
know it?" '

'And he said, "This morning we considered
the evils this land is suffering under at the hands
of men whose aim is the attainment of wealth
and power. To-night we shall look at our own
share in the matter. I think we shall realise that
with us, and not with the men we have lifted up
on high, lies the condemnation." Then his wife
rose and went out, and others followed her; and
the little man's voice rolled among the empty
benches; but he spoke on.'

'And when the service was over he went out.
No elder came to the porch to greet him; but as
he stood there one, he saw not whom, slipped
a leaflet into his hand. He held it up, and read
in the lamplight what was written on it in
pencil. He crushed it up in his hand, as a man
crushes that which has run a poisonous sting
into him; then he dropped it on the earth as a
man drops that he would forget. A fine drizzly
rain was falling, and he walked up the street
with his arms folded behind him, and his head
bent. The people walked up the other side; and
it seemed to him he was alone. But I walked
behind him.'

'And then,' asked Peter, seeing that the stranger was silent, 'what happened to him after that?'

'That was only last Sunday,' said the stranger.

There was silence again for some seconds.

Then Peter said, 'Well, anyhow, at least he didn't die!'

The stranger crossed his hands upon his knees. 'Peter Simon Halket,' he said, 'it is easier for a man to die than to stand alone. He who can stand alone can, also, when the need be, die.'

Peter looked up wistfully into the stranger's face. 'I should not like to die myself,' he said, 'not yet. I shall not be twenty-one till next birthday. I should like to see life first.'

The stranger made no answer.

Presently Peter said, 'Are all the men of your company poor men?'

The stranger waited a while before he answered; then he said, – 'There have been rich men who have desired to join us. There was a young man once; and when he heard the conditions, he went away sorrowful, for he had great possessions.'

There was silence again for a while.

'Is it long since your company was started?' asked Peter.

'There is no man living who can conceive of its age,' said the stranger. 'Even here on this earth it began, when these hills were young, and these lichens had hardly shown their stains upon the rocks, and man still raised himself upwards with difficulty because the sinews in his thighs were weak. In those days, which men reck not of now, man, when he hungered, fed on the flesh of his fellow man and found it sweet. Yet even in those days it came to pass that there was one whose head was higher than her fellows and her thought keener, and, as she picked the flesh from a human skull, she pondered. And so it came to pass the next night, when men were gathered around the fire ready to eat, that she stole away, and when they went to the tree where the victim was bound, they found him gone. And they cried one to another, "She, only she, has done this, who has always said, "I like not the taste of man-flesh; men are too like me; I cannot eat them." "She is mad," they cried; "let us kill her!" So, in those dim, misty times that men reck not of now, that they hardly believe in, that woman died. But in the heads of certain men and women a new thought had taken root; they said, "We also will not eat of her. There is something evil in the taste of human flesh." And ever after, when the flesh-pots were filled with man-flesh, these stood aside, and half the tribe ate human flesh and half not; then, as the years passed, none ate.'

'Even in those days, which men reck not of now, when men fell easily upon their hands and knees, there were of us on the earth. And, if you would learn a secret, even before man trod here, in the days when the dicynodont bent yearningly over her young, and the river-horse which you find now nowhere on earth's surface, save buried in stone, called with love to his mate; and the birds whose footprints are on the rocks flew in the sunshine calling joyfully to one another – even in those days when man was not, the fore-dawn of this kingdom had broken on the earth. And still as the sun rises and sets and the planets journey round, we grow and grow.'

The stranger rose from the fire, and stood upright: around him, and behind him, the darkness stood out.

'All earth is ours. And the day shall come, when the stars, looking down on this little world, shall see no spot where the soil is moist and dark with the blood of man shed by his fellow man; the sun shall rise in the East and set in the West and shed his light across this little globe; and nowhere shall he see man crushed by his fellows. And they shall beat their swords into ploughshares and their spears into pruning hooks: nation shall not lift up sword against nation, neither shall they learn war any more. And instead of the thorn shall come up the fir-tree; and instead of the brier shall come up the myrtle tree: and man shall nowhere crush man on all the holy earth. To-morrow's sun shall rise,' said the stranger, 'and it shall flood these dark kopjes with light, and the rocks shall glint in it. Not more certain is that rising than the coming of that day. And I say to you that even here, in the land where now we stand, where to-day the cries of the wounded and the curses of revenge ring in the air; even here, in this land where man creeps on his belly to wound his fellow in the dark, and where an acre of gold is worth a thousand souls, and a reef of shining dirt is worth half a people, and the vultures are heavy with man's flesh – even here that day shall come. I tell you, Peter Simon Halket, that here on the spot where now we stand shall be raised a temple. Man shall not gather in it to worship that which divides; but they shall stand in it shoulder to shoulder, white man with black, and the stranger with the inhabitant of the land; and the place shall be holy; for men shall say, "Are we not brethren and the sons of one Father?" '

Peter Halket looked upward silently. And the stranger said: 'Certain men slept upon a plain, and the night was chill and dark. And, as they slept, at that hour when night is darkest, one stirred. Far off to the eastward, through his half-closed eyelids, he saw, as it were, one faint line, thin as a hair's width, that edged the hill tops. And he whispered in the darkness to his fellows: "The dawn is coming." But they, with fast-closed eyelids murmured, "He lies, there is no dawn." '

'Nevertheless, day broke.'

The stranger was silent. The fire burnt up in red tongues of flame that neither flickered nor flared in the still night air. Peter Halket crept near to the stranger.

'When will that time be?' he whispered; 'in a thousand years' time?'

And the stranger answered, 'A thousand years are but as our yesterday's journey, or as our watch to-night, which draws already to its close. See, piled, these rocks on which we now stand? The ages have been young and they have grown old since they have lain here. Half that time shall not pass before that time comes; I have seen its dawning already in the hearts of men.'

Peter moved nearer, so that he almost knelt at the stranger's feet: his gun lay on the ground at the other side of the fire.

'I would like to be one of your men,' he said. 'I am tired of belonging to the Chartered Company.'

The stranger looked down gently. 'Peter Simon Halket,' he said, 'can you bear the weight?'

And Peter said, 'Give me work, that I may try.'

There was silence for a time; then the stranger said, 'Peter Simon Halket, take a message to England' – Peter Halket started – 'Go to that great people and cry aloud to it: "Where is the sword was given into your hand, that with it you might enforce justice and deal out mercy? How came you to give it up into the hands of men whose search is gold, whose thirst is wealth, to whom men's souls and bodies are counters in a game? How came you to give up the folk that were given into your hands, into the hand of the speculator and the gamester; as though they were dumb beasts who might be bought or sold?" '

' "Take back your sword, Great People – but wipe it first, lest some of the gold and blood stick to your hand." '

' "What is this, I see! – the sword of the Great People, transformed to burrow earth for gold, as the snouts of swine for earth nuts! Have you no other use for it, Great Folk?" '

' "Take back your sword; and, when you have thoroughly cleansed it and wiped it of the blood and mire, then raise it to set free the oppressed of other climes." '

' "Great Prince's Daughter, take heed! You put your sword into the hands of recreant knights; they will dull its edge and mar its brightness, and, when your hour of need comes and you would put it into other hands, you will find its edge chipped and its point broken. Take heed! Take heed!" '

'Cry to the wise men of England: "You, who in peace and calm in shaded chambers ponder on all things in heaven and earth, and take all knowledge for your province, have you no time to think of this? To whom has England given her power? How do the men wield it who have filched it from her? Say not, What have we to do with folk across the waters; have we not matter enough for thought in our own land? Where the brain of a nation has no time to go, there should its hands never be sent to labour: where the power of a people goes, there must its intellect and knowledge go, to guide it. Oh, you who sit at ease, studying past and future – and forget the present – you have no right to sit at ease knowing nothing of the working of the powers you have armed and sent to work on men afar. Where is your nation's sword – you men of thought?" '

'Cry to the women of England: "You, who repose in sumptuous houses, with children on your knees; think not it is only the rustling of the soft draped curtains, or the whistling of the wind, you hear. Listen! May it not be the far-off cry of those your sword governs, creeping towards you across wide oceans till it pierces even into your inmost sanctuary? Listen!" '

' "For the womanhood of a dominant people has not accomplished all its labour when it has borne its children and fed them at its breast: there cries to it also from over seas and across continents the voice of the child-peoples – "Mother-heart, stand for us!" It would be better for you that your wombs should be barren and that your race should die out; than that you should listen, and give no answer." '

The stranger lifted his hands upwards as he spoke, and Peter saw there were the marks of old wounds in both.

'Cry aloud to the working men and women of England: "You, who for ages cried out because the heel of your masters was heavy on you; and who have said, "We curse the kings that sit at ease, and care not who oppresses the folk, so their coffers be full and their bellies satisfied, and they be not troubled with the trouble of rule"; you, who have taken the king's rule from him and sit enthroned within his seat; is his sin not yours to-day? If men should add but one hour to your day's labour, or make but one fraction dearer the bread you eat, would you not rise up as one man? Yet, what is dealt out to men beyond seas whom you rule wounds you not. Nay, have you not sometimes said, as kings of old: "It matters not who holds out our sword, marauder or speculator, so he calls it ours, we must cloak up the evil it has done!" Think you, no other curses rise to heaven but yours? Where is your sword? Into whose hand has it fallen? Take it quickly and cleanse it!" '

Peter Halket crouched, looking upwards; then he cried: 'Master, I cannot give the message, I am a poor unlearn'd man. And if I should go to England and cry aloud, they would say, "Who is this, who comes preaching to a great people? Is not his mother with us, and a washerwoman; and was not his father a day labourer at two shillings a day?" and they would laugh me to scorn. And, in truth, the message is so long I could not well remember it; give me other work to do.'

And the stranger said, 'Take a message to the men and women of this land. Go, from the Zambesi to the sea, and cry to its white men and women, and say: "I saw a wide field, and in it were two fair beasts. Wide was the field about them and rich was the earth with sweet scented herbs, and so abundant was the pasturage that hardly might they consume all that grew about them: and the two were like one to another, for they were the sons of one mother. And as I looked, I saw, far off to the northward, a speck within the sky, so small it was, and so high it was, that the eye scarce might mark it. Then it came nearer and hovered over the spot where the two beasts fed: – and its neck was bare, and its beak was hooked, and its talons were long, and its wings strong. And it hovered over the field where the two beasts were; and I saw it settle down upon a great white stone; and it waited. And I saw more specks to the northward, and more and more came onward to join him who sat upon the stone. And some hovered over the beasts, and some sharpened their beaks on the stones; and some walked in and out between the beasts' legs. And I saw that they were waiting for something.' "

' "Then he who first came flew from one of the beasts to the other, and sat upon their necks, and put his beak within their ears. And he flew from one to the other and flapped his wings in their faces till the beasts were blinded, and each believed it was his fellow who attacked him. And they fell to, and fought; they gored one another's sides till the field was red with blood and the ground shook beneath them. The birds sat by and watched; and when the blood flowed they walked round and round. And when the strength of the two beasts was exhausted they fell to earth. Then the birds settled down upon them, and feasted; till their maws were full, and their long bare necks were wet; and they stood with their beaks deep in the entrails of the two dead beasts; and looked out with their keen bright eyes from above them. And he who was king of all plucked out the eyes, and fed on the hearts of the dead beasts. And when his maw was full, so that he could eat no more, he sat on his stone hard by and flapped his great wings." '

'Peter Simon Halket, cry to the white men and women of South Africa: "You have a goodly land; you and your children's children shall scarce fill it; though you should stretch out your arms to welcome each stranger who comes to live and labour with you. You are the twin branches of one tree; you are the sons of one mother. Is this goodly land not wide enough for you, that you should rend each other's flesh at the bidding of those who will wet their beaks within both your vitals? – Look up, see, they circle in the air above you!" '

Almost Peter Halket started and looked upward; but there was only the black sky of Mashonaland over his head.

The stranger stood silent looking downward into the fire. Peter Halket half clasped his arms about his knees.

'My master,' he cried, 'how can I take this message? The Dutchmen of South Africa will not listen to me, they will say I am an Englishman. And the Englishmen will say: "Who is this fellow who comes preaching peace, peace, peace? Has he not been a year in the country and he has not a share in a single company? Can anything he says be worth hearing? If he were a man of any sense he would have made five thousand pounds at least." And they will not listen to me. Give me another labour!'

And the stranger said: 'Take a message to one man. Find him, whether he sleep or wake, whether he eat or drink; and say to him: "Where are the souls of the men that you have bought?" '

'And if he shall answer you and say: "I bought no men's souls! The souls that I bought were the souls of dogs!" Then ask him this question, say to him, "Where are the –" '

'And if he cry out, "You lie, you lie! I know what you are going to say. What do I know of envoys? Was I ever afraid of the British Government? It is all a lie!" Then question him no further. But say: "There was a rushlight once. It flickered and flared, and it guttered down, and went out – and no man heeded it: it was only a rushlight." '

' "And there was a light once; men set it on high within a lighthouse, that it might yield light to all souls at sea; that afar off they might see its steady light and find harbour, and escape the rocks." '

' "And that light flickered and flared, as it listed. It went this way and it went that; it burnt blue, and green, and red; now it disappeared altogether, and then it burnt up again. And men, far out at sea, kept their eyes fixed where they knew the light should be: saying, "We are safe; the great light will lead us when we near the rocks." And on dark nights men drifted nearer and nearer; and in the stillness of the midnight they struck on the lighthouse rocks and went down at its feet." '

' "What now shall be done to that light, in that it was not a rushlight; in that it was set on high by the hands of men, and in that men trusted it? Shall it not be put out?" '

'And if he shall answer, saying, "What are men to me? they are fools, all fools! Let them die!" – tell him again this story: "There was a streamlet once: it burst forth from beneath the snow on a mountain's crown; and the snow made a cove over it. It ran on pure and blue and clear as the sky above it, and the banks of snow made its cradle. Then it came to a spot where the snow ended; and two ways lay before it by which it might journey; one, on the mountain ridges, past rocks and stones, and down long sunlit slopes to the sea; and the other, down a chasm. And the stream hesitated: it twirled and purled, and went this way and went that. It *might* have been, that it would have forced its way past rocks and ridges and along mountain slopes, and made a path for itself where no path had been; the banks would have grown green, and the mountain daisy would have grown beside it; and all night the stars would have looked at their faces in it; and down the long sunny slopes the sun would have played on it by day; and the wood dove would have built her nest in the trees beside it; and singing, singing, always singing, it would have made its way at last to the great sea, whose far-off call all waters hear." '

' "But it hesitated. – It might have been, that, had but some hand been there to move but one stone from its path, it would have forced its way past rocks and ridges, and found its way to the great sea – it might have been! But no hand was there. The streamlet gathered itself together, and (it might be, that it was even in its haste to rush onwards to the sea!) – it made one leap into the abyss." '

' "The rocks closed over it. Nine hundred fathoms deep, in a still, dark pool it lay. The green lichen hung from the rocks. No sunlight came there, and the stars could not look down at night. The pool lay still and silent. Then, because it was alive and could not rest, it gathered its strength together, through fallen earth and broken debris it oozed its way silently on; and it crept out in a deep valley; the mountains closed it around. And the streamlet laughed to itself, "Ha, ha! I shall make a great lake here; a sea!" And it oozed, and it oozed, and it filled half the plain. But no lake came – only a great marsh – because there was no way outwards, and the water rotted. The grass died out along its edges; and the trees dropped their leaves and rotted in the water; and the wood dove who had built her nest there flew up to the mountains, because her young ones died. And the toads sat on the stones and dropped their spittle in the water; and the reeds were yellow that grew along the edge. And at night, a heavy, white fog gathered over the water, so that the stars could not see through it; and by day a fine white mist hung over it, and the sunbeams could not play on it. And no man knew that once the marsh had leapt forth clear and blue from under a hood of snow on the mountain's top: aye, and that the turning of one stone might have caused that it had run on and on, and mingled its song with the sea's song for ever." '

The stranger was silent for a while.

Then he said, 'Should he answer you and say, "What do I care! What are coves and mountain tops to me? Gold is real, and the power to crush men within my hand"; tell him no further.'

'But if by some chance he should listen, then, say this one thing to him, clearly in the ear, that he may not fail to hear it: "The morning may break grey, and the mid-day be dark and stormy; but the glory of the evening's sunset may wash out for ever the remembrance of the morning's dullness, and the darkness of the noon." So that all men shall say, "Ah, for the beauty of that day!" – For the stream that has once descended there is no path upwards. – *It is never too late for the soul of a man.*'

'And if he should laugh, and say: "You fool, a man may remake himself entirely before twenty; he may re-shape himself before thirty; but after forty he is fixed. Shall I, who for forty-three years have sought money and power, seek for anything else now? You want me to be Jesus Christ, I suppose! How can I be myself and another man?" Then answer him: "Deep in the heart of every son of man lies an angel; but some have their wings folded. Wake yours! He is larger and stronger than another man's; mount up with him!" '

'But if he curses you, and says, "I have eight millions of money, and I care neither for God nor man!" – then make no answer, but stoop and write before him.' The stranger bent down and wrote with his finger in the white ashes of the fire. Peter Halket bent forward, and he saw the two words the stranger had written.

The stranger said: 'Say to him: "Though you should seek to make that name immortal in this land; and should write it in gold dust, and set it with diamonds, and cement it with human blood, shed from the Zambesi to the sea, yet –." ' The stranger passed his foot over the words; Peter Halket looked down, and he saw only a bed of smooth white ashes where the name had been.

The stranger said: 'And if he should curse yet further, and say, "There is not one man nor woman in South Africa I cannot buy with my money! When I have the Transvaal, I shall buy God Almighty Himself, if I care to!" '

'Then say to him this one thing only, "*Thy money perish with thee!*" and leave him.'

There was a dead silence for a moment. Then the stranger stretched forth his hand. 'Yet in that leaving him, remember; – It is not the act, but the will, which marks the soul of the man. He who has crushed a nation sins no more than he who rejoices in the death throe of the meanest creature. The stagnant pool is not less poisonous drop for drop than the mighty swamp, though its reach be smaller. He who has desired to be and accomplish what this man has been and accomplished, is as this man; though he have lacked the power to perform. Nay, remember this one thing more: – Certain sons of God are born on earth, named by men Children of Genius. In early youth each stands at the parting of the way and chooses; he bears his gift for others or for himself. But forget this never, whatever his choice may be; that there is laid on him a burden that is laid not on others – all space is open to him, and his choice is infinite – and if he falls beneath it, let men weep rather than curse, for he was born a Son of God.'

There was silence again. Then Peter Halket clasped his arms about the stranger's feet. 'My master,' he cried, 'I dare not take that message. It is not that men may say, "Here is Trooper Peter Halket, whom we all know, a man who kept women and shot niggers, turned prophet." But it is, that it is true. Have I not wished –' and Peter Halket would have poured out all his soul; but the stranger prevented him.

'Peter Simon Halket,' he said, 'is it the trumpet which gives forth the call to battle, whether it be battered tin or gilded silver, which boots? Is it not the call? What and if I should send my message by a woman or a child: shall truth be less truth because the bearer is despised? Is it the mouth that speaks or the word that is spoken which is eternal? Nevertheless, if you will have it so, go, and say, "I, Peter Halket, sinner among you all, who have desired women and gold, who have loved myself and hated my fellow, I –" ' The stranger looked down at him, and placed his hand gently on his head. 'Peter Simon Halket,' he said, 'a harder task I give you than any which has been laid upon you. In that small spot where alone on earth your will rules, bring there into being the kingdom to-day. Love your enemies; do good to them that hate you. Walk ever forward, looking not to the right hand or the left. Heed not what men shall say of you. Succour the oppressed; deliver the captive. If thine enemy hunger, feed him; if he is athirst give him drink.'

A curious warmth and gladness stole over Peter Halket as he knelt; it was as, when a little child, his mother folded him to her: he saw nothing more about him but a soft bright light. Yet in it he heard a voice cry, 'Because thou hast loved mercy – and hated oppression –'

When Trooper Peter Halket raised himself, he saw the figure of the stranger passing from him. He cried, 'My Master, let me go with you.' But the figure did not turn. And, as it passed into the darkness, it seemed to Peter Halket that the form grew larger and larger: and as it descended the further side of the kopje it seemed that for one instant he still saw the head with a pale, white light upon it: then it vanished.

And Trooper Peter Halket sat alone upon the kopje.

II

It was a hot day. The sun poured down its rays over the scattered trees, and stunted bush, and long grass, and over the dried up river beds. Far in the blue, so high the eye could scarcely mark them, vultures were flying southward, where forty miles off kraals had been destroyed and two hundred black carcasses were lying in the sun.

Under a group of tall straggling trees among the grass and low scrub, on the banks of an almost dried up river bed, a small camp had been pitched.

The party had lost their mules, and pending their recovery had already been there seven days. The three cart loads of provisions they were conveying to the large camp were drawn up under the trees and had a sail thrown across them to form a shelter for some of the men; while on the other side of the cleared and open space that formed the camp, a smaller sail was thrown across two poles forming a rough tent; and away to the left, a little cut off from the rest of the camp by some low bushes, was the bell-shaped tent of the Captain, under a tall tree. Before the bell-shaped tent stood a short stunted tree; its thick white stem gnarled and knotted; while two stunted misshapen branches, like arms, stretched out on either side.

Before this tree, up and down, with his gun upon his arm, his head bent and his eyes fixed on the ground, while the hot sun blazed on his shoulders, walked a man.

Three or four fires were burning about the camp in different parts, three cooking the mealies and rice which formed the diet of the men, their stock of tinned meats having been exhausted; while the fourth, which was watched by a native boy, contained the more appetising meal of the Captain.

Most of the men were out of camp; the coloured boys having gone to fetch the mules which had been discovered in the hills a few miles off, and were expected to arrive in the evening; and the white men had gone out to see what game they could bring down with their guns to flavour the mealie pots, or to reconnoitre the country; though all native habitations had been destroyed within a radius of thirty miles, and the land was as bare of black men as a child's hand of hair; and even the beasts seemed to have vanished.

In the shade of the tent, formed of the canvas across two posts, lay three white men, whose work it was to watch the pots and guard the camp. They were all three Colonial Englishmen, and lay on the ground on their stomachs, passing the time by carrying on a desultory conversation, or taking a few whiffs, slowly, and with care, from their pipes, for tobacco was precious in the camp.

Under some bushes a few yards off lay a huge trooper, whose nationality was uncertain, but who was held to hail from some part of the British Isles, and who had travelled round the world. He was currently reported to have done three years' labour for attempted rape in Australia, but nothing certain was known regarding his antecedents. He had been up on guard half the night, and was now taking his rest lying on his back with his arm thrown over his face; but a slight movement could be noted in his jaw as he slowly chewed a piece of tobacco; and occasionally when he turned it round the mouth opened, and disclosed two rows of broken yellow stumps set in very red gums.

The three Colonial Englishmen took no notice of him. Two, who were slowly smoking, were of the large and powerful build, and somewhat loose set about the shoulders, which is common among Colonial Europeans of the third generation, whether Dutch or English, and had the placidity and general good temper of expression which commonly marks the Colonial European who grows up beyond the range of the cities. The third was smaller and more wiry and of an unusually nervous type, with aquiline nose, and sallow hatchet face, with a somewhat discontented expression. He was holding forth, while his companions smoked and listened.

'Now what I say is this,' he brought his hand down on the red sand; 'here we are with about one half teaspoon of Dop given us at night, while he has ten empty champagne bottles lying behind his tent. And we have to live on the mealies we're convoying for the horses, while he has pati and beef, and lives like a lord! It's all very well for the regulars; they know what they're in for, and they've got gentlemen over them anyhow, and one can stomach anything if you know what kind of a fellow you've got over you. English officers are gentlemen, anyhow; or if one was under Selous now –'

'Oh, Selous's a *man!*' broke out the other two, taking their pipes from their mouths.

'Yes, well, that's what I say. But these fellows, who couldn't do as farmers, and couldn't do as shopkeepers, and God knows what else; and their friends in England didn't want to have them; they're sent out here to boss it over us! It's a damned shame! Why, I want to know, amn't I as good as any of these fellows, who come swelling it about here? Friends got money, I suppose!' He cast his sharp glance over towards the bell tent. 'If they gave us real English officers now –'

'Ah!' said the biggest of his companions,

who, in spite of his huge form, had something of the simplicity and good nature of a child in his handsome face; 'it's because you're not a big enough swell, you know! He'll be a colonel, or a general, before we've done with him. I call them all generals or colonels up here; it's safest, you know; if they're not that to-day they will be to-morrow!'

This was intended as a joke, and in that hot weather, and in that dull world, anything was good enough to laugh at: the third man smiled, but the first speaker remained serious.

'I only know this,' he said, 'I'd teach these fellows a lesson, if any one belonging to me had been among the people they left to be murdered here, while they went gallivanting to the Transvaal. If my mother or sister had been killed here, I'd have taken a pistol and blown out the brains of the great Panjandrum, and the little ones after him. Fine administration of a country, this, to invite people to come in and live here, and then take every fighting man out of the country on a gold hunting marauding expedition to the Transvaal, and leave us to face the bitter end. I look upon every man and woman who was killed here as murdered by the Chartered Company.'

'Well, Jameson only did what he was told. He had to obey orders, like the rest of us. He didn't make the plan, and he's got the punishment.'

'What business had he to listen? What's all this fine administration they talk of? It's six years since I came to this country, and I've worked like a nigger ever since I came, and what have I, or any men who've worked hard at real, honest farming, got for it? Everything in the land is given away for the benefit of a few big folks over the water or swells out here. If England took over the Chartered Company tomorrow, what would she find? – everything of value in the land given over to private concessionaires – they'll line their pockets if the whole land goes to pot! It'll be the jackals eating all the flesh off the horse's bones, and calling the lion in to lick the bones.'

'Oh, you wait a bit and you'll be squared,' said the handsome man. 'I've been here five years and had lots of promises, though I haven't got anything else yet; but I expect it to come some day, so I keep my mouth shut! If they asked me to sign a paper, that Mr. Over-the-Way' – he nodded towards the bell tent – 'never got drunk or didn't know how to swear, I'd sign it, if there was a good dose of squaring to come after it. I could stand a good lot of that sort of thing – squaring – if it would only come my way.'

The men laughed in a dreary sort of way, and the third man, who had not spoken yet, rolled round on to his back, and took the pipe from his mouth.

'I tell you what,' said the keen man, 'those of us up here who have got a bit of land and are trying honestly and fairly to work, are getting pretty sick of this humbugging fighting. If we'd had a few men like the Curries and Bowkers of the old days up here from the first, all this would never have happened. And there's no knowing when a reason won't turn up for keeping the bloody thing on or stopping it off for a time, to break out just when one's settled down to work. It's a damned convenient thing to have a war like this to turn on and off.'

Slowly the third man keeled round on to his stomach again: '*Let resignation wait. We fight the Matabele again to-morrow,*' he said, sententiously.

A low titter ran round the group. Even the man under the bushes, though his eyes were still closed and his arm across his face, let his mouth relax a little, and showed his yellow teeth.

'I'm always expecting,' said the big handsome man, 'to have a paper come round, signed by all the nigger chiefs, saying how much they love the B.S.A. Company, and how glad they are the Panjandrum has got them, and how awfully good he is to them; and they're going to subscribe to the brazen statue. There's nothing a man can't be squared to do.'

The third man lay on his back again, lazily examining his hand, which he held above his face. 'What's that in the Bible,' he said, slowly, 'about the statue, whose thighs and belly were of brass, and its feet of mud?'

'I don't know much about the Bible,' said the keen man, 'I'm going to see if my pot isn't boiling over. Won't yours burn?'

'No, I asked the Captain's boy to keep an eye on it – but I expect he won't. Do you put the rice in with the mealies?'

'Got to; I've got no other pot. And the fellows don't object. It's a tasty variety, you know!'

The keen-faced man slouched away across the square to where his fire burnt; and presently the other man rose and went, either to look at his own pot or sleep under the carts; and the large Colonial man was left alone. His fire was burning satisfactorily about fifty feet off, and he folded his arms on the ground and rested his forehead on them, and watched lazily the little black ants that ran about in the red sand, just under his nose.

A great stillness settled down on the camp. Now and again a stick cracked in the fires, and the cicadas cried aloud in the tree stems; but except where the solitary paced up and down before the little flat-topped tree in front of the captain's tent, not a creature stirred in the whole camp: and the snores of the trooper under the bushes might be heard half across the camp.

The intense mid-day heat had settled down.

At last there was the sound of someone

breaking through the long grass and bushes which had only been removed for a few feet round the camp, and the figure of a man emerged bearing in one hand a gun, and in the other a bird which he had shot. He was evidently an Englishman, and not long from Europe, by the bloom of the skin, which was perceptible in spite of the superficial tan. His face was at the moment flushed with heat; but the clear blue eyes and delicate features lost none of their sensitive refinement.

He came up to the Colonial, and dropped the bird before him. 'That is all I've got,' he said.

He threw himself also down on the ground, and put his gun under the loose flap of the tent.

The Colonial raised his head; and without taking his elbows from the ground took up the bird. 'I'll put it into the pot; it'll give it the flavour of something except weevilly mealies'; he said, and fell to plucking it.

The Englishman took his hat off, and lifted the fine damp hair from his forehead.

'Knocked up, eh?' said the Colonial, glancing kindly up at him. 'I've a few drops in my flask still.'

'Oh, no, I can stand it well enough. It's only a little warm.' He gave a slight cough, and laid his head down sideways on his arm. His eyes watched mechanically the Colonial's manipulation of the bird. He had left England to escape phthisis; and he had gone to Mashonaland because it was a place where he could earn an open-air living, and save his parents from the burden of his support.

'What's Halket doing over there?' he asked suddenly, raising his head.

'Weren't you here this morning?' asked the Colonial. 'Didn't you know they'd had a devil of a row?'

'Who?' asked the Englishman, half raising himself on his elbows.

'Halket and the Captain.' The Colonial paused in the plucking. 'My God, you never saw anything like it!'

The Englishman sat upright now, and looked keenly over the bushes where Halket's bent head might be seen as he paced to and fro.

'What's he doing out there in this blazing sun?'

'He's on guard,' said the Colonial. 'I thought you were here when it happened. It's the best thing I ever saw or heard of in my whole life!' He rolled half over on his side and laughed at the remembrance. 'You see, some of the men went down into the river, to look for fresh pools of water, and they found a nigger, hidden away in a hole in the bank, not five hundred yards from here! They found the bloody rascal by a little path he tramped down to the water, trodden hard, just like a porcupine's walk. They got him in the hole like an aardvark,[8] with a bush over the mouth, so you couldn't see it.

He'd evidently been there a long time, the floor was full of bones of fish he'd caught in the pool, and there was a bit of root like a stick hal gnawed through. He'd been potted, and got two bullet wounds in the thigh; but he could walk already. It's evident he was just waiting till we were gone, to clear off after his people. He'd got that beastly scurvy look a nigger gets when he hasn't had anything to eat for a long time.'

'Well, they hauled him up before the Captain, of course; and he blew and swore, and said the nigger was a spy, and was to be hanged to-morrow; he'd hang him to-night, only the big troop might catch us up this evening, so he'd wait to hear what the Colonel said; but if they didn't come he'd hang him first thing to-morrow morning, or have him shot, as sure as the sun rose. He made the fellows tie him up to that little tree before his tent, with riems[9] round his waist, and a riem round his neck.'

'What did the native say?' asked the Englishman.

'Oh, he didn't say anything. There wasn't a soul in the camp could have understood him if he had. The coloured boys don't know his language. I expect he's one of those bloody fellows we hit the day we cleared the bush out yonder; but how he got down that bank with his leg in the state it must have been, I don't know. He didn't try to fight when they caught him; just stared in front of him – fright, I suppose. He must have been a big strapping devil before he was taken down.'

'Well, I tell you, we'd just got him fixed up, and the Captain was just going into his tent to have a drink, and we chaps were all standing round, when up steps Halket, right before the Captain, and pulls his front lock – you know the way he has? Oh, my God, my God, if you could have seen it! I'll never forget it to my dying day!' The Colonial seemed bursting with internal laughter. 'He begins, "Sir, may I speak to you?" in a formal kind of way, like a fellow introducing a deputation; and then all of a sudden he starts off – oh, my God, you never heard such a thing! It was like a boy in Sunday-school saying up a piece of Scripture he's learnt off by heart, and got all ready beforehand, and he's not going to be stopped till he gets to the end of it.'

'What did he say,' asked the Englishman.

'Oh, he started, how did we know this nigger was a spy at all; it would be a terrible thing to kill him if we weren't quite sure; perhaps he was hiding there because he was wounded. And then he broke out that, after all, these niggers were men fighting for their country; we would fight against the French if they came and took England from us; and the niggers were brave men, "please sir" – (every five minutes he'd pull his forelock, and say, "please sir!") – "and if we have to fight against them we ought to remember they're fighting for freedom; we shouldn't shoot wounded prisoners when they were black if we wouldn't shoot them if they were white!" And then he broke out pure unmitigated Exeter Hall! You never heard anything like it! All men were brothers, and God loved a black man as well as a white; Mashonas and Matabeli were poor ignorant folk, and we had to take care of them. And then he started out, that we ought to let this man go; we ought to give him food for the road, and tell him to go back to his people, and tell them we hadn't come to take their land but to teach them and love them. "It's hard to love a nigger, Captain, but we must try it; we must try it!" – And every five minutes he'd break out with, "And I think this is a man I know, Captain; I'm not sure, but I think he comes from up Lo Magundis way!" – as if any born devil cared whether a bloody nigger came from Lo Magundis or anywhere else! I'm sure he said it fifteen times. And then he broke out, "I don't mean that I'm better than you or anybody else, Captain; I'm as bad a man as any in camp, and I know it." And off he started, telling us all the sins he'd ever committed; and he kept on, "I'm an unlearned, ignorant man, Captain; but I must stand by this nigger; he's got no one else!" And then he says – "If you let me take him up to Lo Magundis, sir, I'm not afraid; and I'll tell the people there that it's not their land and their women that we want, it's them to be our brothers and love us. If you'll only let me go, sir, I'll go and make peace; give the man to me, sir!" ' The Colonial shook with laughter.

'What did the Captain say?' asked the Englishman.

'The Captain; well, you know the smallest thing sets him off swearing all round the world; but he just stood there with his arms hanging down at each side of him, and his eyes staring, and his face getting redder and redder: and all he could say was, "My Gawd! my Gawd!" I thought he'd burst. And Halket stood there looking straight in front of him, as though he didn't see a soul of us all there.'

'What did the Captain do?'

'Oh, as soon as Halket turned away he started swearing, but he got the tail of one oath hooked on to the head of another. It was nearly as good as Halket himself. And when he'd finished and got sane a bit, he said Halket was to walk up and down there all day and keep watch on the nigger. And he gave orders that if the big troop didn't come up to-night, that he was to be potted first thing in the morning, and that Halket was to shoot him.'

The Englishman started: 'What did Halket say?'

'Nothing. He's been walking there with his gun all day.'

The Englishman watched with his clear eyes

the spot where Halket's head appeared and disappeared.

'Is the nigger hanging there now?'

'Yes. The Captain said no one was to go near him, or give him anything to eat or drink all day: but –' The Colonial glanced round where the trooper lay under the bushes; and then lowering his voice added, 'This morning, a couple of hours ago, Halket sent the Captain's coloured boy to ask me for a drink of water. I thought it was for Halket himself, and the poor devil must be hot walking there in the sun, so I sent him the water out of my canvas bag. I went along afterwards to see what had become of my mug; the boy had gone, and there, straight in front of the Captain's tent, before the very door, was Halket letting that bloody nigger drink out of my mug. The riem was so tight round his neck he couldn't drink but slowly, and there was Halket holding it up to him! If the Captain had looked out! W–h–e–w! I wouldn't have been Halket!'

'Do you think he will try to make Halket do it?' asked the Englishman.

'Of course he will. He's the Devil in; and Halket had better not make a fuss about it, or it'll be the worse for him.'

'His time's up to-morrow evening!'

'Yes, but not to-morrow morning. And I wouldn't make a row about it if I was Halket. It doesn't do to fall out with the authorities here. What's one nigger more or less? He'll get shot some other way, or die of hunger, if we don't do it.'

'It's hardly sport to shoot a man tied up neck and legs,' said the Englishman; his finely drawn eyebrows contracting and expanding a little.

'Oh, they don't feel, these niggers, not as we should, you know. I've seen a man going to be shot, looking full at the guns, and falling like that! – without a sound. They've no feeling, these niggers; I don't suppose they care much whether they live or die, not as we should, you know.'

The Englishman's eyes were still fixed on the bushes, behind which Halket's head appeared and disappeared.

'They have no right to order Halket to do it – and he will *not* do it!' said the Englishman slowly.

'You're not going to be such a fool as to step in, are you?' said the Colonial, looking curiously at him. 'It doesn't pay. I've made up my mind never to speak whatever happens. What's the good? Suppose one were to make a complaint now about this affair with Halket, if he's made to shoot the nigger against his will; what would come of it? There'd be half-a-dozen fellows here squared to say what headquarters wanted – not to speak of a fellow like that' – turning his thumb in the direction of the sleeping trooper – 'who are paid to watch. I believe he reports on the Captain himself to the big headquarters. All one's wires are edited before they go down; only what the Company wants to go, go through. There are many downright good fellows in this lot; but how many of us are there, do you think, who could throw away all chance of ever making anything in Mashonaland, for the sake of standing by Halket; even if he had a real row with the Company? I've a great liking for Halket myself, he's a real good fellow, and he's done me many a good turn – took my watch only last night, because I was off colour; I'd do anything for him in reason. But, I say this flatly, I couldn't and wouldn't fly in the face of the authorities for him or anyone else. I've my own girl waiting for me down in the Colony, and she's been waiting for me these five years. And whether I'm able to marry her or not depends on how I stand with the Company: and I say, flatly, I'm not going to fall out with it. I came here to make money, and I mean to make it! If other people like to run their heads against stone walls, let them: but they mustn't expect me to follow them. This isn't a country where a man can say what he thinks.'

The Englishman rested his elbows on the ground. 'And the Union Jack is supposed to be flying over us.'

'Yes, with a black bar across it for the Company,' laughed the Colonial.

'Do you ever have the nightmare?' asked the Englishman suddenly.

'I? Oh yes, sometimes'; he looked curiously at his companion; 'when I've eaten too much, I get it.'

'I always have it since I came up here,' said the Englishman. 'It is that a vast world is resting on me – a whole globe: and I am a midge beneath it. I try to raise it, and I cannot. So I lie still under it – and let it crush me!'

'It's curious you should have the nightmare so up here,' said the Colonial; 'one gets so little to eat.'

There was a silence: he was picking the little fine feathers from the bird, and the Englishman was watching the ants.

'Mind you,' the Colonial said at last, 'I don't say that in this case the Captain was to blame; Halket made an awful ass of himself. He's never been quite right since that time he got lost and spent the night out on the kopje. When we found him in the morning he was in a kind of dead sleep; we couldn't wake him; yet it wasn't cold enough for him to have been frozen. He's never been the same man since; queer, you know; giving his rations away to the coloured boys, and letting the other fellows have his dot of brandy at night; and keeping himself sort of apart to himself, you know. The other fellows think he's got a touch of fever on, caught wandering about in the long grass that day. But I don't think it's that; I think it's being alone in the veld that's got hold of him. Man, have you ever been out like that, alone in the veld, night and day, and not a soul to speak to? I have; and I tell you, if I'd been left there three days longer I'd have gone mad or turned religious. Man, it's the nights, with the stars up above you, and the dead still all around. And you think, and think, and think! You remember all kinds of things you've never thought of for years and years. I used to talk to myself at last, and make believe it was another man. I was out seven days: and he was only out one night. But I think it's the loneliness that got hold of him. Man, those stars are awful; and that stillness that comes toward morning!' He stood up. 'It's a great pity, because he's as good a fellow as ever was. But perhaps he'll come all right.'

He walked away towards the pot with the bird in his hand. When he had gone the Englishman turned round on to his back, and lay with his arm across his forehead.

High, high up, between the straggling branches of the tree, in the clear, blue African sky above him, he could see the vultures flying southward.

*　　*　　*

THAT evening the men sat eating their suppers round the fires. The large troop had not come

113

up; and the mules had been brought in; and they were to make a start early the next morning.

Halket was released from his duty, and had come up, and lain down a little in the background of the group who gathered round their fire.

The Colonial and the Englishman had given orders to all the men of their 'mess' that Halket was to be left in quiet, and no questions were to be asked him; and the men, fearing the Colonial's size and the Englishman's nerve, left him in peace. The men laughed and chatted round the fire, while the big Colonial ladled out the mealies and rice into tin plates, and passed them round to the men. Presently he passed one to Halket, who lay half behind him leaning on his elbow. For a while Halket ate nothing, then he took a few mouthfuls; and again lay on his elbow.

'You are eating nothing, Halket,' said the Englishman, cheerily, looking back.

'I am not hungry now,' he said. After a while he took out his red handkerchief, and emptied carefully into it the contents of the plate; and tied it up into a bundle. He set it beside him on the ground, and again lay on his elbow.

'You won't come nearer to the fire, Halket?' asked the Englishman.

'No, thank you, the night is warm.'

After a while Peter Halket took out from his

belt a small hunting knife with a rough wooden handle. A small flat stone lay near him, and he passed the blade slowly up and down on it, now and then taking it up, and feeling the edge with his finger. After a while he put it back in his belt, and rose slowly, taking up his small bundle and walked away to the tent.

'He's had a pretty stiff day,' said the Colonial. 'I expect he's glad enough to turn in.'

Then all the men round the fire chatted freely over his concerns. Would the Captain stick to his word to-morrow? Was Halket going to do it? Had the Captain any right to tell one man off for the work, instead of letting them fire a volley? One man said he would do it gladly in Halket's place, if told off; why had he made such a fool of himself? So they chatted till nine o'clock, when the Englishman and Colonial left to turn in. They found Halket asleep, close to the side of the tent, with his face turned to the canvas. And they lay down quietly that they might not disturb him.

At ten o'clock all the camp was alseep, excepting the two men told off to keep guard; who paced from one end of the camp to the other to keep themselves awake; or stood chatting by the large fire, which still burnt at one end.

In the Captain's tent a light was kept burning all night, which shone through the thin canvas sides, and shed light on the ground about; but, for the rest, the camp was dead and still.

By half-past one the moon had gone down, and there was left only a blaze of stars in the great African sky.

Then Peter Halket rose up; softly he lifted the canvas and crept out. On the side furthest from the camp he stood upright. On his arm was tied his red handkerchief with its contents. For a moment he glanced up at the galaxy of stars over him; then he stepped into the long grass, and made his way in a direction opposite to that in which the camp lay. But after a short while he turned, and made his way down into the river bed. He walked in it for awhile. Then after a time he sat down upon the bank and took off his heavy boots and threw them into the grass at the side. Then softly, on tip-toe, he followed the little footpath that the men had trodden going down to the river for water. It led straight up to the Captain's tent, and the little flat-topped tree, with its white stem, and its two gnarled branches spread out on either side. When he was within forty paces of it, he paused. Far over the other side of the camp the two men who were on guard stood chatting by the fire. A dead stillness was over the rest of the camp. The light through the walls of the Captain's tent made all clear at the stem of the little tree; but there was no sound of movement within.

For a moment Peter Halket stood motionless; then he walked up to the tree. The black man hung against the white stem, so closely bound to it that they seemed one. His hands were tied to his sides, and his head drooped on his breast. His eyes were closed; and his limbs, which had once been those of a powerful man, had fallen away, making the joints stand out. The wool on his head was wild and thick with neglect, and stood out roughly in long strands; and his skin was rough with want and exposure.

The riems had cut a little into his ankles; and a small flow of blood had made the ground below his feet dark.

Peter Halket looked up at him; the man seemed dead. He touched him softly on the arm; then shook it slightly.

The man opened his eyes slowly, without raising his head; and looked at Peter from under his weary eyebrows. Except that they moved they might have been the eyes of a dead thing.

Peter put up his fingers to his own lips – 'Hus–h! hus–h!' he said.

The man hung torpid, still looking at Peter.

Quickly Peter Halket knelt down and took the knife from his belt. In an instant the riems that bound the feet were cut through; in another he had cut the riems from the waist and neck: the riems dropped to the ground from the arms, and the man stood free. Like a dazed dumb creature, he stood, with his head still down, eyeing Peter.

Instantly Peter slipped the red bundle from his arm into the man's passive hand.

'Ari-tsemaia! Hamba! Loup! Go!' whispered Peter Halket; using a word from each African language he knew. But the black man still stood motionless, looking at him as one paralysed.

'Hamba! Sucka! Go!' he whispered, motioning with his hand.

In an instant a gleam of intelligence shot across the face; then a wild transport. Without a word, without a sound, as the tiger leaps when the wild dogs are on it, with one long, smooth spring, as though unwounded and unhurt, he turned and disappeared into the grass. It closed behind him; but as he went the twigs and leaves cracked under his tread.

The Captain threw back the door of his tent. 'Who is there?' he cried.

Peter Halket stood below the tree with the knife in his hand.

The noise roused the whole camp: the men on guard came running; guns were fired: and the half-sleeping men came rushing, grasping their weapons. There was a sound of firing at the little tree; and the cry went round the camp, 'The Mashonas are releasing the spy!'

When the men got to the Captain's tent, they saw that the nigger was gone; and Peter Halket was lying on his face at the foot of the tree; with his head turned towards the Captain's door.

There was a wild confusion of voices! 'How

many were there?' 'Where have they gone to now?' 'They've shot Peter Halket!' – 'The Captain saw them do it' – 'Stand ready, they may come back any time!'

When the Englishman came, the other men, who knew he had been a medical student, made way for him. He knelt down by Peter Halket.

'He's dead,' he said, quietly.

When they had turned him over, the Colonial knelt down on the other side, with a little hand-lamp in his hand.

'What are you fellows fooling about here for?' cried the Captain. 'Do you suppose it's any use looking for foot marks after all this tramping! Go, guard the camp on all sides!'

'I will send four coloured boys,' he said to the Englishman and the Colonial, 'to dig the grave. You'd better bury him at once; there's no use waiting. We start first thing in the morning.'

When they were alone, the Englishman uncovered Peter Halket's breast. There was one small wound just under the left bosom; and one on the crown of the head; which must have been made after he had fallen down.

'Strange, isn't it, what he can have been doing here?' said the Colonial; 'a small wound, isn't it?'

'A pistol shot,' said the Englishman, closing the bosom.

'A pistol –'

The Englishman looked up at him with a keen light in his eye.

'I told you he would not kill that nigger. – See – here –' He took up the knife which had fallen from Peter Halket's grasp, and fitted it into a piece of the cut leather that lay on the earth.

'But you don't think –' The Colonial stared at him with wide open eyes; then he glanced round at the Captain's tent.

'Yes, I think that – Go and fetch his greatcoat; we'll put him in it. If it is no use talking while a man is alive, it is no use talking when he is dead!'

They brought his great-coat, and they looked in the pockets to see if there was anything which might show where he had come from or who his friends were. But there was nothing in the pockets except an empty flask, and a leathern purse with two shillings in, and a little hand-made two-pointed cap.

So they wrapped Peter Halket up in his great-coat, and put the little cap on his head.

And, one hour after Peter Halket had stood outside the tent looking up, he was lying under the little tree, with the red sand trodden down over him, in which a black man and a white man's blood were mingled.

ALL the rest of the night the men sat up round the fires, discussing what had happened, dreading an attack.

But the Englishman and the Colonial went to their tent, to lie down.

'Do you think they will make any inquiries?' asked the Colonial.

'Why should they? His time will be up to-morrow.'

'Are you going to say anything?'

'What is the use?'

They lay in the dark for an hour, and heard the men chatting outside.

'Do you believe in a God?' said the Englishman, suddenly.

The Colonial started: 'Of course I do!'

'I used to,' said the Englishman; 'I do not believe in your God; but I believed in something greater than I could understand, which moved in this earth, as your soul moves in your body. And I thought this worked in such wise, that the law of cause and effect, which holds in the physical world, held also in the moral: so, that the thing we call justice, ruled. I do not believe it any more. There is no God in Mashonaland.'

'Oh, don't say that!' cried the Colonial, much distressed. 'Are you going off your head, like poor Halket?'

'No; but there is no God,' said the Englishman. He turned round on his shoulder, and said no more: and afterwards the Colonial went to sleep.

BEFORE dawn the next morning the men had packed up the goods, and started.

By five o'clock the carts had filed away; the men rode or walked before and behind them; and the space where the camp had been was an empty circle; save for a few broken bottles and empty tins, and the stones about which the fires had been made, round which warm ashes yet lay.

Only under the little stunted tree, the Colonial and the Englishman were piling up stones. Their horses stood saddled close by.

Presently the large trooper came riding back. He had been sent by the Captain to ask what they were fooling behind for, and to tell them to come on.

The men mounted their horses to follow him; but the Englishman turned in his saddle and looked back. The morning sun was lighting up the straggling branches of the tall trees that had overshadowed the camp; and fell on the little stunted tree, with its white stem and outstretched arms; and on the stones beneath it.

'It's all that night on the kopje!' said the Colonial, sadly.

But the Englishman looked back. 'I hardly know,' he said, 'whether it is not better for him now, than for us.'

Then they rode on after the troop.

NOTES

1. Kopje, a little hillock.
2. Kraal, a native encampment.
3. Veld, open country.
4. Cape Smoke, a very inferior brandy made in the Cape.
5. Vatje of Old Dop, a little cask of Cape brandy.
6. 'By this shall all men know that ye are My disciples, if ye have love one to another.'
7. The Afrikander Bond, the organised Dutch political party, through whom Mr. Rhodes worked, and by whom he was backed.
8. Aardvark, the great ant-eater.
9. A riem, a thong of undressed leather.

A note on the making of this book

This book has been set in 12 on 14 point Baskerville,
a typeface designed by the English typefounder and
printer John Baskerville (1706-1775) of Birmingham.
Set, printed and bound by National Book Printers Ltd.
Elsies River, Cape.